I0818860

AFTERNOON HOURS OF A HERMIT

ALSO BY PATRICK COTTRELL

Sorry to Disrupt the Peace

AFTERNOON HOURS OF A HERMIT

A Novel

PATRICK COTTRELL

An Imprint of HarperCollins*Publishers*

HarperCollins books may be purchased for educational, business, or sales promotional use. For information, please email the Special Markets Department at SPsales@harpercollins.com.

hc.com

FIRST EDITION

Designed by Renata De Oliveira
Photograph on page 1 courtesy of the author

Library of Congress Cataloging-in-Publication Data has been applied for.

ISBN 978-0-06-343506-3

26 27 28 29 30 LBC 5 4 3 2 1

For SG

AFTERNOON HOURS OF A HERMIT

1

Five years ago I put on my detective hat and my existential black turtleneck in order to solve the mystery of his suicide. I mean the reasons my youngest brother killed himself and his thoughts leading up to his plan. The black turtleneck turned out to be a perfect fit and after sifting and sorting through his belongings, I closed my investigation with satisfactory results. Although we were left with some lingering questions, a few loose ends, some wasted hours here and there, brief and average-length stretches of total mediocrity, paths leading nowhere, mental and emotional cul-de-sacs, overall, everything regarding my investigation turned out okay, THE END.

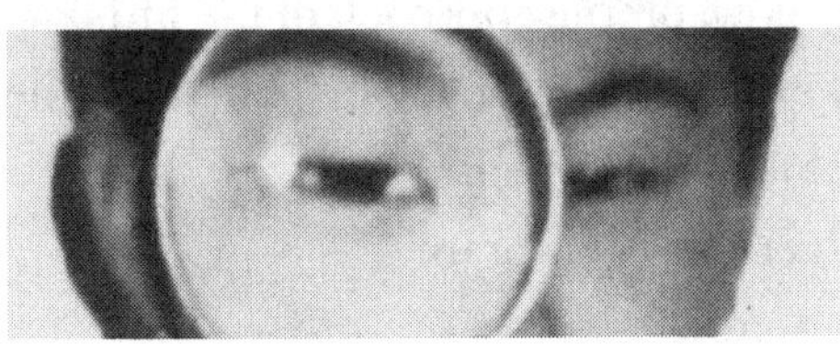

For five years I believed it was over, and then out of the blue I received an envelope with a photo of my youngest brother from our childhood and nothing else. For reasons unclear to me, someone had mailed me a photo in which my now-dead brother is wearing a trench coat, a lanyard with two keys, and a thick black strap around his neck. He must be about eight or nine years old. Attached to the strap is an expensive-looking camera. He's holding a magnifying glass up to his right eye and smiling. A gentle, sincere smile. Sticking out of the trench coat pocket is the corner of a white piece of paper. Paper, keys, camera, magnifying glass, trench; he is a mélange of detective-novel clues and tropes. The trench is the same color as the wall, pale beige with warm yellow undertones. My brother blends into the background like the passive observer he once was and always would be. Until he wasn't. The person in the picture has no idea what he will go on to do one day, the devastation of his plan. When we were little, we played detective together. He was the one who investigated and I was the criminal, the one who left behind breadcrumbs, escaped at the last second, and evaded all consequences. Who could have predicted almost three decades later our roles would be reversed? What stood out to me was his right eye, enlarged from the magnifying glass. *An eye of inquiry.* I sat on my couch, plagued by uneasy speculations. Who had sent this to me? Why now, on the approach of the fifth anniversary of his death? I examined the envelope. There was no return address, no name of the sender.

Only a memento of Moran.

2

That afternoon I was getting ready to teach my troubled youth at the private arts college. Although I had designed a meticulous syllabus, the troubled youth in my creative writing workshop did not want to talk about reading or writing. Instead they spoke at length about their suffering, and I tried to teach them how to take their suffering and the suffering of the people around them and turn it into seemingly coherent prose, semi-digestible, but the troubled youth didn't care, they were too overcome with their own sorrows and depression. And who did I think I was, trying to teach the troubled youth how to write? If someone had asked, even though no one ever asked, I would say I was Dan Moran, a Korean adoptee, single, approaching forty, once plain in appearance as a woman, now ugly as a man, that's who or what I thought I was.

Most importantly, I was no longer useless, I was a writer.

I congratulated myself: five years in the post-suicide phase. It had been five years since I had received the phone call informing me of my youngest adoptive brother's death, permanently and decisively altering the structure of my brain. During those five years, I pursued an MFA in creative writing, I wrote, I taught my troubled youth at a private arts college, I procrastinated, I philosophized, I transitioned, etc. While in graduate school, I transcribed into a book the initial discoveries I had made during the investigation of my brother's suicide: *Sorry to Disrupt the Peace* by ______ Moran. By publishing one book and four or five prose poems, I had transformed myself from no one into an active participant in a thriving intellectual and artistic community: in other words, the contemporary-literature and adjunct-teaching scene in Brooklyn.

Then the photo of my brother appeared in my mailbox, whispering, I am not done with you.

I caught myself staring at the assemblage of mysterious objects in the photo: paper, camera, trench, glass. I was overtaken with a fragile curiosity, I could see myself opening the suicide door again and peering around the suicide frame, just a quick nothing-glance around the suicide doorway to see what's there. I considered calling my Korean adoptee therapist Tina to discuss the strange appearance of the photo in my mailbox, then I remembered she had recently asked me to stop leaving her voicemails unless there was an absolute emergency. Who else could I call? My mother and I hadn't spoken in a year.

Her phone rang three times, and I was surprised when she picked up. I said hello, but I was met with silence.

Who is this? she said at last.

Her voice was curt and sharp, as if she were talking to a telemarketer. It was clear she hadn't recognized my voice.

It's your son, I said.

Matthias? she said.

It's me, Dan.

Oh. Okay.

. . .

In her fragile, halting Midwestern accent, she said she hoped I was calling because I had good news or something positive to share. Without delay, I asked if she or my father had sent me a photo of my youngest brother in the mail.

He must be eight or nine years old, I said. The best years of his life.

She and my father were too busy getting their house ready to send anything in the mail, she said. Getting ready for what, she did not specify, and before she could go on about the status of their house preparations, I asked if she remembered the photo of my brother dressed up as a detective and she said no, she didn't think so, but I sensed an opening, a door left ajar, and I suggested we retrace our steps. Could we go back to the night my youngest brother died, the night he was in the hospital hooked up to the machines, suspended between life and death? After all, she had never told me what had happened in any detail, and I wanted to know what she remembered.

. . .

I suppose there is one thing I haven't thought about in a long time, she admitted.

And I wasn't sure what prompted this divulgence after all these years, if she had forgotten whom she was talking to, Dan Moran, the metaphysical investigator, the one who takes their suffering, ruminates, and writes. She plowed ahead without thinking of the consequences and described to me the way she had held my youngest brother's hand at the hospital that night, how his hand felt surprisingly small, shrunken and soft, less like a human hand and more like *a withered red apple.*

Although she was known in our family as the most forgetful person on the planet, my mother was now describing with perfect recall how a nurse kept coming into the room to see if she or my father needed coffee or water. My mother said she didn't want any coffee or water because that would mean she'd have to let go of my brother's withered red apple, which she clasped firmly between her own hands. She strained her voice to pray and begged God to bring my brother back to life, any kind of life, it just needed to be a life, life, alive, living. My father insisted she drink some water, and when she let go of my brother's hand to accept a paper cone from the nurse, she noticed there was a black smudge on her palm. Wondering where it came from, she looked again at my brother's hand and realized he had written something on his fingers in black marker. Index, middle, and ring.

It was strange, she was saying to me now on the phone.

As she examined his hand more closely, although some of the letters were smudged, she could make out the names of *three women.*

Three women, she said to me on the phone. He had written the names of three women on his hand.

What names? I asked. Whose names?

Why was she telling me this only now?

It was a long time ago, she said. I think one of the names could have been mine, but I might be wrong. I've blocked the others out.

. . .

Could there have been a Beth? she said. Is that possible? Was there a Beth in his life?

There's always a Beth, I said calmly, rationally.

Listen honey, why don't you call your brother Matthias? she said.

When she said the phrase *your brother Matthias* my skin froze, her voice was a wind blowing down the sides of an ice mountain.

Don't you want to talk with Matthias? she said.

Matthias, I thought, the one who's still alive.

I don't want to talk with Matthias, I said.

I was upset.

She's upset!! I could hear my mother whisper to someone, probably my father.

I didn't bother to correct her. My head was already spinning all kinds of stories. The three names started to take possession of my brain. The three names in black marker on his fingers, three exactly, three the magical number of fairy tales from long, long ago, and all of it began with three orphans from Korea, my youngest brother, the middle one, and me.

If I had seen three names of women smudged on his fingers, I would've been haunted by them for the rest of my life, whereas my mother initially withheld from me what she had seen and then she set it aside, five years went by, and she let the image go, she dissolved it, she allowed something better to replace it because she wanted it to be over, she wanted to be done with it. She wanted to throw my brother's withered red apple into the trash or compost it with the worms and the dirt and the grass and the hay.

But it wasn't over.

A suicide is never over.

That's what my mentor Thomas Bernhard had said.

Years ago when I told him during office hours I had solved the mystery of my brother's suicide, he stared at a spot above my head and said a suicide is never over. Suicide is continuous, he warned me. Your brother's suicide is a small river that flows into a big river. Suicide is a river that will never dry up. And now I will tell you a joke, Thomas Bernhard said. He told me a joke, I remembered, but I didn't remember it.

If a mind can keep thinking, it will ruminate, reanimate, and bring back the same old story, adding new angles, fresh diversions, complexities, intrigues, etc. That's what the mind does, Thomas Bernhard said: it drives one mad until one is swaddled in bandages of solitude.

That's not me, I said to no one. My mind was as clear and cold as the rivers of suicide Thomas Bernhard once described for me.

Do you remember that café you used to work at when you were in high school? I heard my mother saying. The owner has been helping us get ready.

Get ready for what, exactly? I said.

My mother hesitated, then said she and my father were hosting a get-together with relatives on the fifth anniversary of my youngest brother's death.

We weren't sure if you would want to come. You must have other plans, she said. It's just a memorial dinner, that's all. It's okay if you can't attend.

I had already marked the date itself in my Google Calendar under events: *SEPT 28 my youngest brother's suicide.* I was free the rest of the day. She said she didn't want to put any pressure on me to attend the dinner, as she assumed I was busy working almost a thousand miles away in Brooklyn. She must have forgotten how helpful it could be to have a metaphysical investigator and writer hanging around the scene, asking questions, searching for clues, and amassing them into great big balls of theories and hypotheses regarding the taking of one's own life without warning, it must've slipped my parents' minds, they had other things to think about, whereas, until I transitioned, all I had was my brother's suicide, in fact, my brother's suicide was the main source of my life material. If I didn't have his suicide—and not just any plain old suicide but the tragic suicide of a Korean adoptee—what exactly did I have?

. . .

Are you listening, ______? I said your father wants to talk with you, my mother said.

I heard muffled voices, then she must have handed my father the phone because his voice exclaimed that I was upsetting my mother, I was retraumatizing her with my questions, and I should talk to Matthias if I wanted to take a stroll down memory lane. He said if my brother wasn't available to talk, I should go through my high school yearbook, flip it open to a random page, close my eyes, and point at a person to reach out to on LinkedIn. Before I could ask him about the photo that had appeared in my mailbox, I heard him promise he would pray for me, he would pray for me to find a new cause, a new obsession and devotion, maybe even God himself. Could I look around and find God? He hung up.

Whenever my parents asked if I could find God, I pictured my mother walking around the house, calling out, Yoo-hoo,

God, where are you? Dinner's almost ready!! If I had to be obsessed with someone or something, why couldn't it be God? What was wrong with God, after all he had done for me and my orphan brothers? Now, when I closed my eyes and tried to look around and find God, all I could see were the smudges on my youngest brother's fingers in black marker. The three names. Blurred, fuzzy black caterpillar squiggles trembling, coming back to life, yes, back to life, life can be so beautiful, I could hear my mother at the hospital saying to no one, life is always worth living, didn't he know that? Why didn't he know that? And as the black caterpillars threatened to overtake my tranquility, here I was on the threshold, about to go back to look into the matter, about to get sucked into the past, which was at odds with the forward momentum of my transition, ruminating on the mystery of how and why the names ended up where they did.

I halted my preparations to teach the troubled youth, and I began to pack my carry-on suitcase with my necessary writing materials. *We weren't sure if you would want to come. You must have other plans.* And although it might have been a grave error to return to the ones who refused to acknowledge who and what I had transformed myself into, against my better judgment, on September 25, I purchased a plane ticket to Milwaukee.

I folded the envelope with the photo and tucked it into my carry-on suitcase. And then it occurred to me: the envelope was addressed to my deadname. Whoever had sent it was a person of interest from my past; they didn't want to let it go.

3

On the night of September 26, the plane landed. As the Uber approached my childhood home in the suburbs of Milwaukee, I called the chair of the English department at the private arts college to tell him I would be unavailable to teach my troubled youth for at least a week, as I had decided to take time off to attend the memorial dinner of my youngest brother's death. *Let the youth teach one another* was one of my teaching strategies, thanks to Thomas Bernhard. Although it was ten at night, eleven the chair's time, I left a simple voicemail explanation for the chair: I've gone back to hell for a while, I explained, perhaps he would appreciate the heads-up.

While at my childhood home for the memorial dinner, my plan was to work on my manuscript in progress. I would utilize my parents' house as my private writing residency, since the refrigerator would be stocked, meals would be prepared by my mother and her sisters, and I'd have my childhood bedroom all to myself; I could work without distraction on my manuscript in progress, my character study. It was a psychological thriller. I was writing my psychological thriller in my head the way my mentor Thomas Bernhard had taught me, all I had to do was sit at a desk, preferably the desk in my childhood bedroom, drink coffee, enter a state of mental tranquility, and write it down. Thomas Bernhard said you must write the story in your head before you put down a single word, if you start off with the wrong sentence, the wrong syntax, the wrong silence, the entire foundation will crumble later on. Thomas Bernhard said writing isn't writing, writing is playing the piano; that's how literature is made. So far I had twelve pages.

Is there anyone else you could talk to about what you're going through right now? I could hear my Korean adoptee therapist Tina asking me while taking tiny delicate sips of herbal tea out of a ceramic mug.

No, Tina, unfortunately not, I said to no one.

There's not one other person you could talk to? If you really try to think about it for a while?

Of course I had numerous contacts in my phone, such as *Marco Weed* and *Jan Plumber*, but even after I had become an instructor and mentor of numerous troubled youth at the private arts college in Brooklyn, all of whom were at least ten percent more depressed and suicidal than I was but eighty percent wealthier and better dressed, even after I was welcomed with open arms into a burgeoning intellectual and seemingly philosophical contemporary literature and adjunct-teaching scene and culture, I did not have many friends or people to talk to, not one real friend, I thought sadly as I stepped out of the Uber and dragged my carry-on suitcase down the curving driveway toward the side entrance where I could enter the house unobserved, my preferred status in life: unobserved, not-there, no, nothing. My parents had installed around the perimeter of the house a metal latticework gate in *an Oriental style*. Horrified, I unlatched it and peered into the mudroom window of my childhood home hoping to catch a glimpse of who was inside, hoping to see a friendly face, although I wasn't sure who that would be.

You must have friends, I heard my Korean adoptee therapist Tina say, besides Jan Plumber and Marco Weed. You know, real friends, not people who do things for you or sell you stuff. Friendship has been a form of poison to me, I thought as I tried to picture my friends, especially my writer friends. I kept trying to picture them, my writer friends from the contemporary literature and adjunct scene in Brooklyn. No, the writer friends I pictured only reminded me of the palpable anxiety and awkwardness I felt whenever I interacted with them. Years ago at a literary reading, I overheard a writer friend say to another writer friend: ______ *Moran is the most anxious person I have ever met.* The other writer friend agreed immediately. Perhaps part of the problem was I had surrounded myself with the fiction writers instead of the poets. I had chosen the wrong world to immerse myself in; the poets were nightclub docents of mourning and melancholia and the fiction writers were real estate agents. No, I don't think I have one real *writer friend* who's alive, all of the writer friends I can confide in are dead writers, my true friends, the physically dead ones who go on living in my brain, after all, it's easier to be friends with a dead writer because they're no longer striving toward anything, they're dead, those are the only ones who are important to me, the non-strivers, besides Thomas Bernhard, who's obviously still alive, but he's not a writer friend per se, he would be horrified to be thought of as a writer or as a friend.

I approached the side entrance of my parents' house, more than three thousand square feet of airless, sunless rooms more suitable for a morgue, if the morgue were a house located on a dead-end street at the bottom of a tree-shaded hill with a stone castle motif, a barn turret, a decorative wagon wheel, leaf-choked gutters, backed-up pipes clogged with dead skin, hair, little black-green caviar blobs of life material, a small corporate-looking fountain made of steel and concrete that was shut off its first winter and never restored to its full-on foam-spouting capabilities, a citadel of suburban Midwestern taste and Catholicism with *an Oriental gate*, once filled with the laughter and tears of three orphans from Korea, mostly tears, mostly mine because of unpredictable hormonal imbalances and ailments. Your orphans are adorable, I once overheard one of our neighbors say in a singsong voice to my mother. If I had actual musical talent, that's what I would've titled my debut album of contemporary pop piano music, *Your Orphans Are Adorable*, unfortunately I had no musical talent except humming. I was very good at humming, especially whenever my troubled youth at the private arts college in Brooklyn became silent, whenever there was an uncomfortable silence. And there were so many over the span of three hours sitting in a classroom, how could there not be, so I would turn to my humming talents to break the silence, preferably humming something simple by Aphex Twin or Bach or Dvořák. At the beginning of the semester, a student had complained about the way I tended to hum uncontrollably and for much longer than they would have liked to listen to. It led to an encounter with the chair of the English department. I really want to like you, Dan, he told me in the hallway a week ago. But I don't think I can hire you again. This is your last semester.

It must've rained earlier that night because when the trees trembled, raindrops slid off a thousand leaves and frisked my shoulders. I watched my carry-on suitcase roll of its own volition down the sloping pathway past the side entrance. I followed it to the firepit in the backyard where my middle brother Matthias would hide from my parents and smoke weed. Someone had left a coat draped on the back of a canvas chair. I half expected to see Matthias sitting there and I shuddered. It had been years since we had seen each other. Would he call me by my name? Would he acknowledge me as a man? A normal man wouldn't worry about these matters, I said to no one, a normal man would expect to be greeted and acknowledged as a man. The rain-soaked leaves were shaking and the outline of a person emerged from them. It was a man, but it was not my middle brother. He aimed his phone at me, a spotlight on my face as if I were standing on a stage about to deliver a dramatic monologue.

What the fuck? he said. Is that ______ Moran? After all these years?

4

My deadname shocked me back into the present. My old name, my former name was my deadname but it wasn't dead, it would be animated and brought back to life by the people I no longer knew, or the ones who missed my mass email announcement regarding my new name and pronouns, or the ones who chose to utterly ignore my mass email announcement in favor of preserving a version of me they might find more socially palatable. My parents, for example. Perhaps there was a small continent who thought of me, perhaps dreamed of and had nightmares of me, as ______ Moran. Good old ______ Moran who as a figure of people's imaginations, experiences, and memories, would never die. I told the man my new name in an authoritative voice as if it were a command, not a name.

But I've thought of you as THE ______ Moran for almost forty years, he said as he fumbled with his phone.

He shut off the flashlight. Why THE ______ Moran, I wondered, were there other ones I didn't know about? The man who was possibly a cousin or an uncle, I wasn't sure which, now sat across from me. For reasons I didn't want to ruminate on, I had inadvertently avoided my family's eyes and faces for years. He didn't say anything about my physical appearance even though I was hoping, praying he would remark upon my physical appearance and how he no longer recognized me, how I had transformed myself into a completely new person.

Don't you remember me, your uncle Karl? he said. The last time I saw you in person, you were a little girl.

Perhaps it was because we were sitting in the darkness, I speculated, perhaps that was why he didn't say anything about my physical appearance.

I know what you're doing out here, he said. You wanted some privacy, like me, so you could smoke in peace.

He took out a vape from his coat and encouraged me to sit down. I plopped onto the canvas chair and a pool of rain splashed my butt, soaking my pants.

So tell me, he said, what are you really doing back in Milwaukee?

What do you mean? I'm here to attend my youngest brother's memorial dinner.

I didn't say anything about my investigation or my private writing residency. It was too soon. I had twelve pages and hardly any clues, nothing to amass into great big balls of theories and hypotheses.

It's surprising, that's all, Uncle Karl said. Your parents said they didn't know if you'd come. I'm surprised you decided to turn up. Not that I've been around much, either, to be honest.

He laughed. The way he had said *decided to turn up* sounded sarcastic, as if I just happened to be in the area and was dropping in on the festivities casually. I wanted to remind Uncle Karl that five years ago I was the one who had offered my parents emotional and physical support, unlike my brother Matthias, who had refused to come home; certainly I should get some spiritual credit.

What have you been doing all these years? he said.

I've been in and out, I said. In and out of phases of total mental darkness and destruction.

Oh yeah, your parents said you went to grad school.

That's right.

And you turned yourself into a writer, he said. Your book is about your family's tragedy. I didn't read it. Sorry about that.

It's better you didn't.

He said he saw my book on the corner of the street once in Chicago. Someone had left it out in the open in the middle of the street with car after car swerving around it. It was as if someone had flung it to the ground and left it there. He picked it up, examined it, recognized my name, then put it back in the middle of the street. He relayed the sighting to my mother, how he had spotted my book in the middle of the street, and she started sniffling, perhaps her allergies have been acting up, I thought, but the good news, he said, the exciting news, was my parents were moving forward with their lives, literally and metaphorically. I wasn't sure what he meant by that.

They're in the process of buying a new house and selling this one, he said.

No one told me, I said.

No one told me they were fleeing from my childhood home. After all these years. Ideally, they would buy the new house and keep my childhood home as a storage unit. I wondered how their plans would affect my writing residency. Would I still have access to my childhood bedroom? Had they already disposed of my childhood desk and chair? If I don't have the necessary materials and perfect conditions to write, I thought, I will never be able to write anything!!

Maybe they wanted to surprise you with the good news. I assume you've moved on as well, he said.

The dead won't leave us alone, I said to Uncle Karl, they leave behind a residue of clues that can lead us to nothing and other times to a greater place of understanding, those gleaming, gruesome shining jewels, and we refuse to leave the clues alone.

He nodded and asked if I had been in contact with my brother, the one who was still alive. He said Matthias had been working diligently on his speech for months.

His speech? I said.

I was astonished. I had never known Matthias to dedicate himself to any literary pursuit.

What speech? I said. Who invited him to give a speech?

Uncle Karl said that my middle brother was one of the featured speakers of my youngest brother's memorial dinner. According to my mother, Matthias had set aside at least a few hours on nights and weekends for the preparation of his speech.

Not sure he'll able to top last year's speech, though, he said.

Last year's speech?

I wondered what he was referring to.

When I heard the name Matthias, my mind flashed to his face and how he was a Korean like me, like my youngest brother, none of us biologically related. My genes had nothing to do with his face, my genes had nothing to do with the fact that Matthias had never bothered to open the envelope and read the document my youngest brother wrote moments, seconds, even, before he took his own life. Whereas I was the one most eager to read my youngest brother's suicide letter, and had philosophically absorbed its contents as soon as I clicked the document icon on his laptop, monstrously swept clean of all relevant information, Matthias hadn't even bothered to look at the version my parents printed out and sent to him in Los Angeles via priority mail. He kept the letter stuffed at the back of a junk drawer in his kitchen.

Perhaps by now, five years post-suicide, it had been recycled.

I only knew my brother Matthias never bothered to read my youngest brother's suicide letter because his wife, beautiful, outgoing, and naturally maternal, had traveled thousands of miles to my parents' house after my youngest brother's funeral to explain in person why Matthias couldn't be there and to offer her condolences. She spent her days with us cooking, cleaning, dusting, wiping down, and brightening the rooms with her radiance.

What a good daughter you are, my mother had said to her.

She's a daughter-in-law, I clarified from my position on my parents' living room couch, where I sat upright with a pillow on my lap for approximately two or three weeks so I could observe everything and offer my support. And sometime during her stay with us, Matthias's naturally maternal wife, who was in fact pregnant but not yet showing, hypothesized that my brother Matthias was too emotionally devastated to consider opening the letter, and *if he was the man she thought he was*, he would probably remain that way the rest of his life. Trapped inside of an emotional devastation.

She didn't know what kind of man my middle brother was, I said to myself. She would never know unless I told her.

Just as he had skipped attending my brother's funeral, leaving me as the sole support in the wake of my parents' grief, he skipped reading my brother's suicide letter. And I was right about Matthias, I was right to suspect he'd never glanced at it. His wife claimed he couldn't bring himself to read the suicide letter, but she made it sound like a respectable decision, as if Matthias were trying to protect or preserve something sacred in his mind about his relationship with my youngest brother. Our brother. His privacy, perhaps, his infinite solitude. He was preserving my youngest brother's dignity by not reading the suicide letter. But that wasn't right, that couldn't be right, no, the honest truth was Matthias didn't possess the mental or emotional capacity to stare into the gaping void of my brother's suicide letter, and yet he was the more respectable and socially desirable out of the two of us because he was born a male and stayed that way, whereas I was a once-female turning into a male, also, he had impregnated his wife, the outgoing, naturally maternal one who would later give birth to an adorable baby girl, and my parents loved that, they loved people who brought forth goodness into our world by making fresh little babies, popping them hot out of the baby oven, and what was

I, Dan Moran, doing with my body and my genitals? Nothing good. Nothing productive or reproductive.

Did your parents ask *you* to give a speech? Uncle Karl asked.

. . .

So they didn't ask you, he said. Maybe they're waiting to ask you in person.

To soften the blow, he took out his vape and offered it to me.

Take it, he insisted.

He was really overdoing it, I thought. Part of me was surprised my parents hadn't asked me to be a featured speaker, since I was one of their two remaining adoptive children, and the only one who had taken the time to solve the mysteries of his violent and nauseating death. I wondered if their refusal to assign me a role as a featured speaker had something to do with my transition, if they were uncomfortable with my name or how I was starting to look like a youngish Asian man and less like their *dearly beloved daughter*, the androgynous person they had become accustomed to, if slightly confused by, over the years.

Or was it something else?

Was there something I had overlooked?

Are you feeling well? Uncle Karl asked.

. . .

Or have you been feeling not so well? he said.

My parents must've told him about my tendency to feel *not so well*.

I'm okay, I said.

Oh, that's good, Uncle Karl said. I was worried I had said something to upset you.

Truthfully, there's something that's been on my mind.

Oh? What's that? he said.

I was staring at the trees surrounding us, and I swear I could see a black caterpillar inching across the length of a branch even though it was dark out, so dark, it was too dark out to see. I asked if he knew about the three names written on my brother's hand, if he had heard anything.

I remember some rumors floating around, he said. Something about an apartment not far from here. A woman at the funeral who covered her face with her hands, crying. Like she didn't want anyone to see her.

A woman. Crying at a funeral. I tried to imagine who that could be. She could be anyone, I thought. The detail about how she covered her face with her hands seemed important. But why?

I'm trying to think of her name, Uncle Karl continued. Do you remember seeing her?

I didn't want to explain to Uncle Karl how I had missed my brother's funeral. But unlike Matthias's absence, mine was due to a technical mishap, not by choice. I saw a vision of myself driving a black Honda Accord down a pockmarked road, leaning against the steering wheel as I listened intently to a news program on the radio. The bees were dying out, the newspeople said, a sorrowful harbinger of the apocalypse. Suddenly I felt the Honda Accord rumble over a small animal or a pothole, and it bobbed up and down like a ship blown off course by gales of misfortune into an uncharted world.

A world in which I missed my youngest brother's funeral because of a flat tire.

Uncle Karl was already heading back toward my childhood home.

If you have questions about what happened, talk to Matthias, he called out.

5

My youngest brother was dead.

Less than a year after I finished graduate school, I published a novel about my dead brother and I left out the one who was living.

My middle brother Matthias, the one who's still alive.

If I were to write about my youngest brother, I had thought, I would have to write about the middle one, but at the time of my youngest brother's death, the nature of his suicide overwhelmed the subject of the middle brother and what he had done, how he had driven me away. Or had I driven him away?

I don't know, I don't know, I don't know, I told my Korean adoptee therapist Tina. She told me to stop saying *I don't know* because it was avoidant and dismissive of other people's pain, or perhaps she was tired of me spinning our conversation into corners and alleys, perhaps she was exhausted by my avoidance, and who could blame her? Instead of approaching the open door, I would avoid. In the end it had been easier for me, Dan Moran, to leave Matthias out, to emphasize my familial estrangement and solitude rather than to exploit the conflict between us, since I was already in the process of exploiting the tragedy of my youngest brother's suicide.

I could deal with only one devastation at a time.

To put it plainly, I had to pretend someone who was living

never existed in order to write a book about someone else who was dead.

I made other changes, too.

I changed the date of my youngest brother's death from September 28 to 30 to ensure that my novel was fictional and not a memoir.

I utilized a register of disgust instead of mourning, guilt, regret, etc.

I intensified my ugliness because I was suspicious of writers who insinuated their own physical beauty or sexual charisma.

I hid myself in the form of a menstruating woman, careful to tiptoe around the problem of *my dysphoria*, blissfully ignorant of the ones who might read the book to scrutinize its pages for clues to my dysphoria and subsequent transition, and subject me to some stupid psychoanalytic reading of my character, gender, writing, etc.

Other than that, almost everything was based on fact.

And since then, the more distance I've gained from my authorial decisions, the more I've realized what acts of avoidance they were.

In 2013, in the post-suicide phase, while I was at my childhood home sitting on the wicker basket couch for two or three weeks, observing, offering my emotional support and investigative assistance to my parents during their time of mania and desperation for answers, Matthias was in Los Angeles generating original content for Netflix. My parents said he was too sensitive, too emotional, for the situation at hand. They said he was in a depression, trapped inside his emotional devastation.

They felt sorry for him, they made excuses for him, they said he was brokenhearted over losing his little brother. And what about my broken heart? I said to no one. My middle brother Matthias was known for being calm and rational, whereas I had gained the reputation of volatility and impulsive behavior even though I was more reclusive than impulsive. My parents trusted Matthias's perspective over mine, which I once overheard my father refer to as *somewhat foggy*. Our daughter's perspective can be somewhat foggy, he had said to someone in a room. The last time I talked to Matthias on the phone, five years ago, shortly after my youngest brother's funeral, he said he blamed our parents for my youngest brother's death. He ranted about how he'd had enough of their little white lies and omissions and deceptions over the years. He was sick of their cluelessness, how they had looked the other way instead of homing in on my youngest brother's troubles, instead of intervening, they had turned away, he was exhausted by their devotion to delusional fairy tales, their Catholic devotion to forgetting, to move on and to forgive and forget.

It was strange how I, the helpful observer with a somewhat foggy perspective, would never go on to blame my parents, I would absolve them, I would publicly state to anyone who listened that in no way were the two of them at fault for my youngest brother's suicide.

And it came back to me now how, each year on the anniversary of my youngest brother's death, I would call my parents, and the first year I called them, my mother said a grief counselor told her it was possible she and my father had extended my youngest brother's life; if he had ended up with other adoptive parents, different ones, worse ones, his life might have been even shorter than what it had been, therefore, from a certain angle, it could be said my parents were life extenders, the grief counselor hypothesized, my parents could be proud that the shortness of my brother's life was longer than what it might have been had he been raised by other ones.

When I asked my mother if it could be said that I, too, was a life extender since I had lived alongside him for many years, the phone went quiet, I heard her breathing, then my mother's voice trembled, she said she couldn't be entirely certain. No, she couldn't be certain, she repeated. She couldn't be certain that the only one in the house who had shared my youngest brother's anxiety, depression, suicidal ideation, and obsession with the NBA, the one who once accidentally walked in on him masturbating in his bedroom and instantly walked out, the one who knew and understood him *on a philosophical level*, could have extended his life by a year or two or six to eight months at minimum. She was sorry she couldn't be certain.

If I wasn't a life extender, what was I?

What's that? said my mother.

What was I to him, then? I said. Can you tell me what I was to him?

All I could hear was laughter and the celebratory clinking of glassware and silverware. Had I been interrupting something? Were my parents at a restaurant? My mother refused to answer my question. I repeated, *Can you tell me what I was to him?* I was met with her silence, a silence that would continue to grow throughout the years, *the silence surrounding his suicide*, until at last she spoke up to suggest I call the grief counselor to ask for his opinion on the matter. Do you have his number, honey? she said. I can give it to you. I never called him, even though it bothered me not to be officially stamped as a life extender by the grief counselor. I don't know how we can be sure what we are to anyone, I remembered thinking, even if we ask them directly, there's no way to know. It's a mystery what anyone thinks about another person, but I would reopen my investigation and find out. I had started to persuade myself the names on my dead brother's hand, or something in connection with them, would tell me who or what I was to him.

6

Whenever I returned to my childhood home, I felt as if I were the sole survivor of an apocalyptic event, like the protagonist in *Wittgenstein's Mistress*—except I'm not menstruating, I'm ruminating. In the mudroom I opened my carry-on suitcase to look for fresh pants, the ones I had on were wet and clung to my skin. It took me longer than I would've liked to remove them as I steadied myself against the wall. Aunt Sue? I heard a woman's voice call out. A cousin came in as I stood in the middle of the mudroom in my underwear. I hadn't seen my cousin Maddie in many years. Oh my God!! Maddie said, then she turned on her heel and ran out. I finished putting my pants on. Someone had taped to a cabinet a crude sketch of a house with a triangle for a roof and, looming above, a hot pink shattered sun. I assumed the artist was my brother Matthias's daughter. Not long after my youngest brother died, my middle brother Matthias's daughter came into the world, and I found this symmetry totally grotesque and appalling, possibly because my parents referred to Matthias's daughter as a blessed gift. God is good!! What timing to receive such a blessed gift.

Inside the cabinet was a pair of navy Adidas flip-flops. I took off my wet shoes and socks and stepped into them. A perfect fit, they molded naturally to the arches of my feet as if I had been wearing them all this time. I could hear my cousin Maddie's voice in another room, alerting my parents to *an Asian male intruder* in the house until Uncle Karl intervened and assured everyone there was no intruder, it was simply ______, their eldest child. My father asked him why I hadn't come directly into the house to greet them. I leaned forward, listening closely. I was ecstatic with joy whenever I had the opportunity to overhear what people said about me as if I weren't there. Whenever I ran out of things to talk about during my creative writing workshop with the troubled youth, I would, without warning, get up from the conference table and wander out into the hallway, where, if I wasn't careful, I could spend the rest of the class eavesdropping on my troubled youth, although they hardly ever said my name. I was nothing to them; they preferred to talk about debt, activism, gender, trauma, etc. I was disappointed when I didn't hear my name come up at all. And then I swore I heard someone in my childhood home refer to me as a *semi-demon*, which jolted me out of my teaching reverie. My father demanded to know what the semi-demon had been doing outside hanging around the firepit the way Matthias loitered when he was a teenager, who did I think I was, some kind of weed-smoking vagrant in the rain? I heard Uncle Karl clarify that the rain had stopped.

We never hear from ______ except when she's in one of her obsessive moods, said my father. She becomes hyperfocused and doesn't see anything except her obsession.

I think it's he, said Uncle Karl. That's what he told me.

She wants us to call her Dan now, added my mother.

For almost forty years we've known her as ______, said my father. So you can imagine how confusing this has been.

He identifies as Dan Moran, said Uncle Karl.

I detached myself from the mudroom wall and advanced

into the kitchen. My mother, my father, Uncle Karl, the three of them stood there with my cousin, mouths opened, their bodies tense and upright as if rigid with a paralyzing fear.

It hadn't occurred to me that they might be afraid of me or what I was turning myself into.

I'm a male detective now, I might have explained to them.

I was surprised to see that in my five-year absence my parents had not succumbed to grief, their wild, debilitating, and radiant grief. Instead it seemed, against all odds, they were thriving. I wondered if this meant my middle brother Matthias was thriving, too. And I didn't like to think about how the circumstances might appear from their perspective, how this *once-female-now-male* estranged family member *semi-demon* who had come out of nowhere would now install himself in their home, which they were in the process of emptying out and selling. And not only would he install himself there, he would set up the perfect circumstances and conditions in order *to observe and write about them.* No, I didn't like to think about this at all, how perhaps it once was acceptable to drop in on things, to have a quick look-see throughout the house when I was in my mid-thirties, tiptoeing around, picking at metaphorical scabs like a troubled young woman, but now, as a man approaching the wizened age of forty, to turn up this way at a family function, at the last minute possible, might be incredibly inappropriate and weird.

Peculiar. Eccentric. Semi-demonic.

No one moved forward to greet or embrace me. Instead my father was staring at my feet. He asked me why I was wearing flip-flops. I tried to remember if there was some kind of rule about not wearing flip-flops in the house.

What's wrong with wearing flip-flops? I said.

No, it's nothing, he said.

He claimed it didn't matter, although I could tell he was upset. Then all at once I remembered the sound of my youngest brother clomping around the house in his Adidas flip-flops, the flip-flops I was wearing now, slapping against the floor from his bedroom to the kitchen and back, the same circuit, bedroom to kitchen and back, with occasional detours to the bathroom. How could I have forgotten? Perhaps he thought if he wore them, he could trick everyone into thinking he had gone to college and lived and showered in a dorm. His Adidas-flip-flops scheme worked out perfectly, and not only had my parents believed he went to college, they believed he graduated and went on to law school, first the University of Chicago, then Marquette University, then to a federal law enforcement training program in Wyoming via a personal connection forged at the University of Chicago with the attorney general. All his outlandish lies were perpetuated and proliferated by my parents. Had you never thought of visiting him at his so-called dorm? I wanted to ask them. Had you never considered dropping in on him unexpectedly?

Of course, it had never occurred to me, either, I could've dropped in on him even though I lived a thousand miles away in Manhattan and had not at that time fully come into my investigative identity as a detective.

He told us so many lies over the years, where to begin?

My parents were whispering to each other. A cousin

scraped a plate into the sink and turned on the garbage disposal. It became clear no one wanted to pursue the matter of my brother's Adidas flip-flops. My mother turned to me and said she had been saving something special for this occasion. I followed her into the two-story foyer. As she disappeared into a walk-in closet, I noticed the wall of family photos, which had been haphazardly arranged. I didn't want to look at them, I would've preferred to walk past the wall without stopping, because I knew I would be forced to confront several images of who I once was to them, daughter, sister, little girl, stark reminders of what I was.

In the center of the arrangement was a group picture of my father and fellow Catholic school administrators and their families at a staff picnic from more than twenty-five years ago, a group of the whitest people on the planet standing in front of a volleyball net plus my Korean brothers in Umbros and neon-green T-shirts. I was in seventh grade and nowhere to be found. It was possible I had not been invited to the picnic. I scanned the wall for more photos of interest, and as I was about to turn away, my eyes settled on a distinct image. I could hardly believe what I was seeing: the photo of my youngest brother wearing a trench coat, a duplicate of the picture I had in my carry-on suitcase, framed and matted.

My brother's eye of inquiry gazed at me.

When the camera clicked, whom had my youngest brother been gazing back at?

What had he seen?

Since I'd received the photo, it had not occurred to me to ask, Who was the photographer? A family member or a relative? A neighbor or a babysitter? Could it have been Agnes, the one with a cloud of white hair who watched us Thursday nights? I imagined doing a Google search for *Agnes babysitter*, which would result in at least six million hits. Agnes, the one who once dressed me up in a vaguely East Asian red silk outfit with tiny faux-ivory clasps she had brought of her own volition. She lured me outside onto the concrete steps with the promise of a brand-new stuffed animal buffalo, made me pose with it, and photographed me. She said I looked like the sweetest little Asian doll; she would be appalled to see what I'd since turned myself into.

It's possible whoever took the picture had a connection with its sender, perhaps they were the same person, perhaps it was someone in this house. My cousin Fran came into the two-story foyer and asked if I wanted to accompany him to the basement, where we could talk privately. I explained I was not in the right mood. He said he hoped we could talk soon, there was something important he wanted to discuss, but I could not pull myself away from my brother's photo on the wall. He lingered next to me, then gave up. I was enchanted by my brother's smile, how it seemed sincere here, unlike the other photos, in which his smile was less sincere. The picture must've been taken before any illness had surfaced and taken possession of his thoughts, poisoning him against his existence. We're all one sincerely smiling photograph away from being totally poisoned against our own existence, I said or thought.

The high point of my life was probably fourth grade, he once said to me. Or maybe it was third. Who knows.

My mother emerged from the closet and came over to see what I was looking at. I mentioned someone had sent me a duplicate of the detective photo on the wall, without divulging any other aspects of my investigation for fear of jeopardizing it. My mother said she had no idea who the photographer was, it wasn't her or my father. She had always disliked that picture, she explained. She didn't like detectives, she didn't like mysteries, she didn't like stories about people losing things, she didn't like shadows, she didn't like death, etc., and besides, it had a dark aura, and neither she nor my father could bear to look at a photo like that, any kind of photo with him, smiling or not. Since my youngest brother's death, the wall of photos had become incredibly painful for my mother to walk past, emotionally annihilating, and over time, she had numbed herself by pretending it was a blank white wall. A sun-warmed pristine blank white wall inside an art museum, she explained.

And it occurred to me that I myself had walked past this very wall with my brother's detective photo on my way into the kitchen, always from the two-story foyer into the kitchen, for at least a decade I had passed the photo of my detective. Its benign banal beige-ness had not made an impression. And so when I received its duplicate in the mail, it was as if I were seeing it for the first time.

My mind had tricked me.

I had seen this photo thousands of times.

What else had I missed?

Had I overlooked something?

Here's what I've been saving for you, my mother said.

She handed me a packet of letters bundled with a flesh-colored rubber band. Bills and collection notices. She said I could put my suitcase in my childhood bedroom if I didn't mind sharing my bed with Aunt Sue, who had already established herself there, otherwise I could stay in my youngest brother's room if I needed privacy.

What about Matthias's room? I said. Can't I stay in there?

It's reserved, she said.

For Matthias? I said. When is he coming here?

She sifted her hand through a bowl of potpourri on a side table, activating the aroma.

Tonight or tomorrow. Did you know your youngest brother liked this smell? she said. It was his favorite brand of potpourri.

I didn't know he had a favorite brand of potpourri, I admitted.

I had always thought I knew everything about him. This was a new development.

The manufacturer stopped making it, she said, but your father bought a twenty-five-pound bag of it on eBay. It's in the junk room upstairs. We're halfway finished with clearing it out.

The wheels had been set in motion for the sale of the house. I wondered what clues had been destroyed in the process, perhaps heaps of them, then I caught myself in the reflection of a mirrored cabinet, staring blankly at the bowl of potpourri. I tried to imagine what a mass of twenty-five pounds of weightless, pointless potpourri looked like.

You didn't tell me you're selling the house, I said. You never tell me anything.

Of course we told you, said my mother. We don't keep secrets in this house.

We don't keep secrets in this house and we never tell lies, I whispered.

A parental mantra from the deepest recesses of my early childhood.

If you're staying in your brother's room, she said, I'll need to change the sheets.

Even though my youngest brother is no longer freshly dead, I'd rather stay in my room with Aunt Sue, I said.

I knew it was a questionable setup, my staying in the room and sharing a bed with Aunt Sue, considering I was on testosterone and almost *a forty-year-old man*. Aunt Sue came into the two-story foyer, having heard her name from the kitchen.

I can stay in your brother's room, she offered.

My mother thanked her, then asked me if I wanted to say hello to my relatives. I told her it was imperative that I begin to set myself up in my childhood bedroom. I noticed no one had said anything about my appearance or my voice. No one had asked me to give a speech.

Are you going to the hospital with us tomorrow morning? my mother asked.

The hospital? For what? I said.

The two of them looked at me strangely.

A special occasion for your brother.

I pictured Matthias stepping up to a podium, tapping the microphone.

Which brother? I asked.

What do you mean which brother? said my mother. Your youngest brother.

She took a tissue from her pocket and blew her nose.

I'm not sure I can go, I said. I have some work to do.

Work? my mother said, appalled. You brought your work?

I explained I was in an early phase of my manuscript in progress. I explained it had taken me years to begin my psychological thriller, even with the emotional support and encouragement of my mentor Thomas Bernhard. My mentor, my salvation. I had abandoned numerous attempts at other books, for instance, a monologue by a man in a bathtub, ranting about the neighbors who live in the apartment above him. One day he gets out of the bathtub, gets dressed, leaves his apartment to fly to Iowa where he's set to give a talk on the state of the novel. Somehow, the story ends with him inviting a graduate student back to his hotel room. Instead of having sex, the man rants at her about his upstairs neighbors. She listens. He gets drunk and hits his head on the edge of the nightstand, THE END. I explained I tried to write a book about an Asian man who looks out a blue window, titled *The Blue Window*. I explained I once wasted a year working on a novel from the perspective of a nonhuman, specifically a bumblebee, in the act of taking an enormous shit on a very thick white carpet at a writers' conference in Los Angeles. Exhausted, I gave up after a hundred pages; I was surprised I had gotten that far, *but I still had so much further to go.* A few years and nothing to show for all my troubles but the beginning of my psychological thriller, perhaps ten or twelve pages at most, the first ten or twelve pages are the easiest to write, I once said to Thomas Bernhard during office hours, the first ten or twelve pages are effortless, seamless, boundless effortlessness; it's the rest of it that's completely insufferable. It never opens up the way I want it to, I explained to my mother and Aunt Sue. I only wanted to conjure a latticework of light and tranquility, but because of my limitations, I always end up suffocated in a broom closet of despair.

My mother blew her nose into the tissue, tears in her eyes. Aunt Sue gave her a fresh tissue. My mother asked me if I was writing about our family again. It was the first time she had acknowledged I had written and published a book. We never talked about my writing, we talked only about my teaching; teaching was customer service and volunteer social work. She was always comfortable with charity, sacrifice, the poor and needy. Writing was art, and she wasn't comfortable with art. Art was not community service. Art was not a pan of meat loaf to feed the hungry. She was much more comfortable talking about my teaching, the most feminine of customer service jobs.

Well, are you? my mother said. Are you writing about us again?

First I observed them, then I wrote about them, then I hated myself for writing about them. Of course I had always considered the real-life effects of fiction or what literature could do to the people depicted in my writing. Even in my psychological thriller, my character study; I didn't want to injure anyone with *my opulent and elegant depictions of reality.*

I lied and said, No, of course not, why would I do that?

Aunt Sue spoke up and it sounded like she said, Well, what else do you have to write about, then?

I could hardly believe my ears!!

I'm writing a psychological thriller, I said.

About what, though? Aunt Sue said.

It took me a long time to say anything. I wasn't good at thinking on my feet or coming up with new concepts and ideas on the fly.

A lost man, I said at last. I'm writing about a lost man.

7

In my childhood bedroom there was a stack of thick paperbacks on my desk with pastel covers of serene mountain landscapes, quaint castles, and billowing white clouds. The paperbacks belonged to my mother, who was a member of a monthly book club for elderly women. I couldn't imagine what they talked about each month, perhaps they didn't talk, perhaps they prayed. I picked up one of the paperbacks and read the back cover: *How do you live in the aftermath of a betrayal? An old man in a village will take the negative events from the fabric of his life and spin them into something positive which will determine the fate of his village and save the desperate people who surround him.* What cheap vulgarity was my mother reading? I decided the book must be Christian fiction. I couldn't believe what a doorstopper it was, more than five hundred pages. How could a person write five hundred pages of this banal vulgarity and I could hardly get to one hundred pages about my little bumblebee pooping on the rug?

I opened my closet. Aunt Sue's shirts and dresses were hanging up, gauzy, flowing silks in an array of patterns, colors, and swirls. My childhood bedroom, once a bastion of austerity and elegance, was no longer recognizable to me with her feminine textures. My bed was in the corner of the room where it had been for as long as I could remember. My parents hadn't bothered to empty out my childhood desk. There was a small file box in one of the drawers with pictures, letters, my youngest brother's Pope Pius High School yearbook, and my notebooks. My mother had emailed me a photo of the box a few months ago, asking if she should throw it away. I should've realized then they were clearing out the house, moving on literally and metaphorically, damaging potential clues in the process. She had a history of rummaging through my things, picking through my closet and scoping out what was under the bed, that was how she discovered my copy of Judy Blume's *Forever* when I was in fourth grade, I had highlighted the sex scenes and hidden it under the bed. What is this trash you're looking at? she said as she flipped through the pages. When I was younger, I was under her constant surveillance. One weekend she came to visit me at my dorm in Iowa for a weekend and couldn't keep herself from reading my notebook, where I had recorded the height of a bridge for Introduction to Physics. Later that day she took me to Panera Bread for a special lunch, *just the two of us*, she said, even though I wasn't sure who else she would've invited, since she had traveled alone and she didn't know my friends. In the vinyl booth, as we picked at our salads, she asked me with a sad, serious expression if I was interested in the heights of bridges and most importantly why, if it had something to do with how I was feeling, if recording the heights of bridges in my notebook had anything to do with my emotional temperature, as if I were researching the heights of bridges for a secret suicide plan. If I wanted to die, I explained calmly to my mother as we sat in the vinyl booth at Panera Bread, the last thing I would do is step off a bridge. I would rather step off a chair, a coffee table, or a plastic stool than step off a bridge!! Throughout my entire life, she suspected I was harboring special suicide plans, and she interpreted my behavior based on that suspicion. Little did she know, she picked the wrong one to be suspicious of. If only she had trained her suspicious, paranoid suicide-gaze onto my youngest brother, the antisocial one, the one in a lifelong clinical depression, the one who refused to go to high school for several months, instead of me, the detective, the one who was a helpful person, a reliable person, a straight-A student, who had tried to commit suicide half-heartedly just once or twice, who knows where we'd be today!! Paranoid people are correct that there's always something to be paranoid about, I thought, only sometimes they pick the wrong thing. The most important thing about being paranoid is to make sure one picks the right thing, the right person, the right situation to be paranoid about. Most days paranoia pays off, I said to myself. When my mother emailed me about the box in my childhood desk drawer, she was insinuating she had already combed through my materials in a forensic manner. Too much knowledge about a person can be a dangerous thing, I thought, sometimes it's better not to know anything, or the least amount possible, in order to maintain a functioning relationship. Sometimes it's better not to know anything.

No, that can't be right, I thought.

I would prefer to know everything.

My youngest brother's eye of inquiry came to mind.

The aroma of his favorite potpourri lingered in my nasal passages.

Crushed red berries and apple skins.

I set the bundle of letters my mother had given me on my desk, smaller than I remembered, it was closer to a child's desk from elementary school than anything functional for an adult. I wasn't sure if I would fit into it. Although I was once so thin my mother said I looked like a starving orphan then immediately apologized and asked if it had hurt my feelings since for a brief period I was literally a starving orphan, that was decades ago, and now I was an average size, having gained weight from testosterone. The last time I was in my childhood home, there had been a fresh suicide. Then five years passed, and I believed I had attained a certain clarity about the familial situation that allowed me to be calm, rational, and mindful, practically Buddhist, in my interactions with the Morans. The landline was ringing. Can someone answer the phone? I shouted into the hallway. On the sixth ring, I answered the phone on my bedside table and a voice began speaking.

Hello? a woman said. The woman's voice sounded far away as if she were underwater, her voice was garbled.

Hello, I said.

The woman went on speaking, I swore I heard her say my deadname, something about ______ Moran. A shudder passed through me.

Sister, I thought she said, I'm looking for his sister. Is she at home?

I could visualize the word *sister*, a very dark marble, and how it rolled off her tongue onto the floor.

Rolling, rolling. It would never come to a stop.

Who is this? I said. Do you want to leave a message?

I'm looking for his sister kept echoing in my brain.

There's no one like that here, I said.

. . .

There's no one like that here and there never was!! I said.

I slammed the phone into its cradle. I tried to calm myself. I decided it must be someone playing a practical joke, although the woman seemed to insist upon the sister. I made a mental note to ask my parents if they had received any strange phone calls at night.

A day ago, as I was purchasing my plane ticket to Milwaukee, I wanted nothing more than to sit at my childhood desk and work on my psychological thriller in progress, but now that the moment had presented itself, when all I had to do was go up to the desk, sweep off my mother's Christian fiction paperbacks strewn all over its surface, contort my body to fit its proportions, sit down, and take out my work, I realized the arrangement was wrong.

I pushed my desk across the bedroom to a more strategic, favorable position. I imagined as I worked, I would face the window and surveil the driveway like some kind of striving sentinel-scribe. Compelled by a morbid curiosity, I opened my computer and did a Google search for *Agnes babysitter.* As I had predicted, there were more than six million results. I did another search for *Agnes babysitter Milwaukee obituary*, on the off chance that my former babysitter was dead. If so, had someone from her family gone through her belongings and sent me the photo of my youngest brother, knowing I alone was closest to him? I clicked through several images of elderly women with soft clouds of white hair in the Midwestern fashion, but none of them was the Agnes I once knew.

As I closed my investigation for the night, I heard a car come up the driveway of my childhood home, club music blasting. The driver got out and popped open the trunk. It was too dark to see who it was, even with my face pressed against the glass, I could see only the top of a head, a person with dark hair lit up by the car's headlights which switched off after a moment. I tapped at the window to see if I could get the person to look up and show their face. The person kept their head down. I opened the window to call out to them. It was so quiet I imagined I was living on a dim, damp farm in the middle of nowhere and I could hear the cows and pigs breathing in the barn. Suitcase wheels whirred over the smoothness of the pavement. Before I could call out, the person disappeared into my childhood home, and I wondered if it was my middle brother Matthias.

8

It didn't surprise me that our little brother killed himself, my brother Matthias said to me on the phone five years ago. After all, what did he have to live for?

He was laughing and I joined him. The tasteless way I laughed with my middle brother came back to me as I sat all night at my childhood desk, the way I laughed with him at the idea that my youngest brother didn't have much to live for, and therefore in a certain light, his suicide could be considered a rational decision. I laughed with Matthias and I knew I was making a mockery of my youngest brother and his life. And I thought about how spiritually weak I was back then, long before I met and changed my life under the direction of Thomas Bernhard, the person who altered the course of my life, my writing salvation. How agreeable and willing I was to go along with my brother Matthias's laughter, possibly because a part of me, if it could be said there are parts, was afraid of him.

9

On the morning of September 27, I waited for the coffee to finish brewing.

Having spent every morning in this suburban Milwaukee kitchen for half of my life, all I could remember was the desire to break free from the suburban prison and escape, but now that I had escaped, I had returned of my own volition and attempted to transform the prison into my own private writing residency. All last night I told myself I must sit at my desk and work. I had spent an hour thinking about the first sentence of my manuscript, but nothing else came to me except the image of my youngest brother's withered apple.

The three names on his withered apple skin.

One of them possibly my mother's name, leaving at least two other names unaccounted for.

The black caterpillar names woolly on his skin in the hospital.

What would the eye of inquiry discover about my youngest brother now that five years had passed?

I had not considered the conditions of the house with its attendant death traces might be unsuitable as a place to work on my psychological thriller.

Last night, with my bedroom door closed, I expected at any moment to hear a knock, and even if no one knocked, the expectation of the knock was totally paralyzing. When someone did knock, they knocked at least five or six knocks, then they'd give up and begin to speak to me through the door with the assumption that I was listening and ask me questions about what I was going to do with my time the next few days and if I planned to join them on their hospital excursion. I could hear bits of conversation. Is Noni coming or is she still bedridden? I heard someone else say, the semi-demon has decided to seal himself off from the rest of the world as per usual, but I didn't recognize the voice. The telephone rang persistently throughout the night and no one answered it until six or seven rings. Someone had slipped a note underneath my door. *Are you free today to discuss the state of your finances?* I was confused. I couldn't think of anyone in the house who'd be interested in discussing that.

Growing up in the house, I never paid attention to what anyone else was doing, although someone was always watching television. Certainly my mother could be found sitting somewhere in the depths of the basement sewing a piece of cloth, a gray-and-white embroidered handkerchief that required her total devotion and care. The present-day circumstances of the house and its interruptions took me away from my work on my psychological thriller. For the first time in my adulthood I had free time to write, the entire day ahead of me. I could spend all my time in my childhood bedroom writing, although there was also my work with the troubled youth at the private arts college to consider.

The last text I received was from a troubled youth: *Yo Mr Moran I found out today my mom has brain cancer so I will need an extension on my workshop submission.* My troubled youth never stopped texting me and divulging, and in response to their somewhat upsetting and inappropriate divulgences, I put my phone on the Do Not Disturb setting. There was no one to talk to. In fact, the house was so large and empty-seeming, I could leave my bedroom and walk around and not see or hear anyone even though there were at least five other people, if not more, moving around, doing things, etc.

One must find a distraction while the morning coffee brews or it will take forever, I reflected as I sat at the kitchen table. I turned my attention to the bundle of letters my mother had saved for me. I flipped through the stack, animating my deadname. Letter after letter, such an innocuous name, I couldn't say why it bothered me to see it there in its stark factual plainness as vast and dry as the Sahara. There were notices from collection agencies about unpaid medical bills. I did a brief calculation; somehow I had amassed thousands of dollars in debt without my knowledge, simply by existing.

At the bottom of the pile, I noticed an envelope without a return address. Inside was a handwritten letter.

Dear Ms. ______ Moran,

Did you forget something? You may not know who I am. But I feel as if I know you very well. We are closer than you think. For instance, I know you have many questions that have gone unanswered about a variety of topics near to your heart. If you would like the answers—and I know you :) so of course you would like the answers—I suggest you come to this address: 212 Alexander Lane.

The detective photo of my brother. The names on my brother's hand. The woman who covered her face at the funeral. There must be a correspondence with this letter, I said to no one, a thread of connection. But only realists believe everything in the human enterprise is connected, Thomas Bernhard once warned me during office hours. He said, Realism is a sanctuary for the brainless!!

I stared at the letter, at my deadname with its Sahara dryness. The smiley face :) blinked at me in a menacing and threatening way. I could hear it laughing; it sounded like my brother Matthias's laughter on the phone five years ago. His laughter rang in my ears for days, lingering with me in my brain, *his harassment laughter*.

The envelope did not have a name or return address. According to the postmark, the letter had been sent a couple of weeks ago. I scanned my brain: but what was I doing a couple of weeks ago? I was smoking weed with a few of the troubled youth in the park, unseasonably warm, where we discussed the strength of Fiona Apple's discography. Are you crying? one of them asked me. I'm sweating, I said. I remembered I took a long afternoon nap during which I dreamed of an elevator opening onto the seventh floor of an academic building, the floor enveloped in darkness, an ocean of black waves lapping at my feet, and a tiny white cuticle moon floating above my head. Most likely I ate chips and salsa in the bathtub. Perhaps I went to a reading or made an excuse not to go to a reading. At the bookstore I might have chosen not to go to, I opened and closed a book without remembering a single word I had read, not one word made an impression; that's contemporary fiction, I said to myself.

The coffee machine was beeping. I watched the carafe fill drip by drip and I thought I overheard my middle brother Matthias talking on the phone with someone, but I didn't see him anywhere.

Matthias? I called out. Is that you?

. . .

Silence.

Back in my childhood bedroom with my coffee and the threatening smiley face letter, I returned to the address 212 Alexander Lane. I thought of the people I knew named Alexander. There weren't any. I looked up the address on Google Maps. From the street view perspective, 212 Alexander Lane was an apartment building like all apartment buildings in Milwaukee, two stories, outdated, perhaps from the seventies, planks and shingles of dark brown damp-looking wood, balconies with grim, murky-looking sliding glass doors and cheap plastic blinds, a tipped-over tricycle here or there, clumps of bushes and trees, and a blurred ghost figure stepping out of a vehicle in the parking lot. Perhaps it was a delivery man or a tenant or Agnes the babysitter or a crying woman, it was impossible to tell.

I took a sip of coffee and swirled it in my mouth. It tasted like apples, a mass of withered red apples, oak-barrel-aged.

I zoomed in on the blurred ghost figure from Google Maps, and based on the figure's proportions and longish white hair, I convinced myself it was the outline of a woman, not a man. Then I studied the smiley face letter's handwriting, slightly looping with sensual hills and valleys, and I hypothesized a woman had written it. If the writer was a woman, she might have a connection to the three names on my brother's hand and the crying woman at the funeral.

Suddenly I pictured a constellation of women who had surrounded my youngest brother, although in the twenty-nine years I had known him, I never heard him say a woman's name besides my deadname or Natalie Portman or a teacher or neighbor. I had once written the sentence: *It was possible he was asexual.* I had written another sentence: *He did not dream of women or men.* Four years ago, when I wrote those sentences under the guidance of Thomas Bernhard, I thought they were correct, but now I wasn't sure.

And then I remembered how, shortly after the funeral, sometime in the early stages of the post-suicide phase, my cousin Fran sat next to me on the living room couch, my observation post, and said there was something I should know.

My cousin Fran and my youngest brother had formed an email friendship based on their mutual fandom of a television show about a man who saw into the future and the past, an investigator of serial killings motivated by the occult. At first their email friendship focused on this television show, but over time their discussions delved into the personal. According to Fran, my youngest brother had revealed the story of his relationship with a young woman he had met at his high school. The young woman had struggled with depression and suicidal ideation, experimented with hard drugs, and had been lured into sex work. He said the two of them had fallen in love and made plans to run away together. My brother refused to tell my cousin Fran her name.

Something about my youngest brother's story sounded familiar to me.

Leaving Las Vegas, I said to Fran.

What? he said.

It sounds like the plot from *Leaving Las Vegas*. The book.

I hadn't thought about this in years. I had originally dismissed the story of my youngest brother's supposed girlfriend as some kind of fantasy, as it did not align with what I knew about him. *He did not dream of women or men.* From an early age, I had an intuitive sense about other people and their psychological motivations, I said to no one. Years ago, I explained to Fran how my youngest brother had raided my bedroom closet and stolen my books, numerous books integral to my philosophical formation during my high school years. In addition to *Leaving Las Vegas*, I'd read *Jernigan*, *A Flag for Sunrise*, *Easy in the Islands*, *The Names*. I had a threshold of one hundred: I was interested in a book or a film or an album only if fewer than one hundred people had heard of it. Hypothetical people, I do not personally know one hundred people. In my twenties, I used to smoke clove cigarettes, I explained to my cousin Fran, I would enthrone myself in the second-story window of a carpeted coffeehouse in downtown Milwaukee and read Nietzsche and Adorno on my breaks from working behind the counter. And based on what my cousin Fran told me, it became clear that my youngest brother had picked up some gritty nightlife stories from my existential bookshelf, which I had amassed by spending my days perusing the used bookstores of suburban and downtown Milwaukee. I'd sit on the threadbare carpet with my back against a wooden bookshelf, reading, and I'd casually switch the yellow price stickers from $7.99 to $1.00 by scratching them off with my fingernail and smoothing them back on as if nothing had happened. I'd leave the bookstore with *Leaving Las Vegas*, *Jesus' Son*, *A Confederacy of Dunces*, *American Psycho*, *Under the Volcano*. I saw no way forward except through these books, through the voices of so many white men, men I was both drawn to and repelled by. *Less than Zero*, *Airships*, *The Bushwhacked Piano*, *The Sportswriter*, *A Fan's Notes*, *Suttree*. I believed they could teach me something, my swaggering, sauntering, suicidal white men. Men who chose hell. Men who throw the dog down the ravine all wrong. I don't care anymore about cloves or carpeted coffeehouses. I no longer concern myself with dogs-down-the-ravine levels of destruction. I'm in my reparative phase, I remembered explaining to my cousin Fran. I told him I suspected my brother had lied about his relationship with the young woman. He had conjured her from my existential bookshelf, it was a fiction made out of fiction, I asserted, but my cousin Fran refused to believe my hypothesis, my cousin Fran insisted the young woman was real. My cousin Fran and I stood at a philosophical impasse. He wanted to believe in my youngest brother's fabrications, simple and elegant like fairy tales.

Everyone loves to believe such lies.

My cousin Fran said they had met in high school, but he couldn't remember what year.

Your brother refused to tell me her name, he told me.

What did she look like?

He never described her.

Where is she now? What does she do?

No, no, I don't know anything, my cousin Fran said. And there are no traces of her anywhere.

I detected a sound of desperation in his voice. I wondered if my cousin Fran had searched for her.

How do you find a person like that, a person who fails to leave a single trace?

I remembered a book I had read about a man who needs to find a woman from his past, but he knows nothing about who she is presently. He decides the best way to find her is to drive to the lakeside town where she was last seen, but to abandon his search, his hope of finding her. For months he walks around and talks to people. He stops thinking about her. He stops looking for the woman. One evening he sees her in the middle of town and he goes to talk with her. THE END. But that was a work of fiction, I thought, and I would need to be more proactive. A detective can't simply walk around and look at things. I needed a car. A detective drives around in a car. A detective ventures out into the world and questions random people. A detective must devise a world of possibility through these interactions. There's not much of a difference between a detective and a writer, I reflected, except a writer gives readings.

That morning, with shafts of sunlight streaming through my bedroom window, I came up with the contours of a plan. I would call my youngest brother's high school, Pope Pius, and schedule a reading in memory of my youngest brother. My reading would be designed to draw interest from his former classmates and perhaps his supposed high school girlfriend herself. If not her, someone who once knew her or *knew of her*. After all, a person can't exist on this planet without having left behind some kind of trace, especially a troubled young woman who will always attract the attention of a man. I was betting on the fact that most of his classmates still lived in suburban Milwaukee. Almost everyone who grew up in suburban Milwaukee stayed in suburban Milwaukee. It was cheaper to live in the suburbs of Milwaukee, cheaper and more comfortable than almost anywhere else in the Midwest, and everyone in the suburbs of Milwaukee had been raised on the foundational values of cheapness and comfort. I would invite the ones who had remained, almost all of them, to the high school, and after the reading, I would question them. With a renewed sense of purpose and determination, I called my youngest brother's high school and left a voicemail introducing myself as a published local author.

I have a unique and special proposal for you, please call me back as soon as you can, I said.

I searched for an administrative assistant's email on the high school's *Contact Us* page and forwarded them a few favorable articles from blogs featuring ______ Moran, author of *Sorry to Disrupt the Peace*. I did not bother to explain the discrepancy between my name and the name in the favorable articles; what must simply be accepted should never be explained. And yet what should never be explained and simply accepted is what people fear the most, I thought. I sat and waited a few minutes for my phone to ring. Then I smacked my head. I had forgotten to turn off the Do Not Disturb setting on my phone. I checked my voicemail and discovered I had missed several calls and texts from Aunt Sue.

We're in the Ferrari Wing at the hospital. Everyone's here.

Did you get lost?

Where are you?

What are you doing?

10

My parents kept their keys in a beige lockbox, unlocked, in the mudroom. I found what I was looking for and went into the garage, where my youngest brother's car, his black Honda Accord, sat motionless and silent, like an ancient turtle resting on a rock in a cool damp garden. For five years it had sat there. I was astonished they hadn't sold it. Let it become someone else's car, I thought, let it transform into someone else's memory. If I hadn't been on testosterone, it's possible a tear would've come to my eye and slid down my cheek. They kept his car, I said to no one as I unlocked the door and let myself in. They were moving on literally and metaphorically, according to Uncle Karl, but after all these years, my parents had chosen to hold on to his Adidas flip-flops and his black Honda Accord. Two objects with starring roles in his suicide plan. The car's gray fabric interior looked exactly as I remembered except for the blue-and-yellow high school graduation tassels now hanging from the rearview mirror. I instantly recognized the tassels from my youngest brother's high school. My mother had hung them there. She had gone through box after box of knickknacks during her knickknack-purging phase and had hung them up; she believed the brightness of the tassels shimmering blue and gold would counteract the dark forces of what had occurred in the driver's seat. My youngest brother decided to end his life where I now sat, and as the years went by, my parents must have thought his car would go to waste if they couldn't drive it around town, run some quick errands, etc. They would pick up Uncle Karl from the airport and drive him to their home, and the entire ride from the airport to the suburbs they would make small talk with Uncle Karl and he would sit there totally ignorant of the fact that my mother or my father occupied the seat where my brother chose to take his own life. When they drive his car, they drive my brother, they drive his death site. And here I was, also driving it, on my way to the hospital, where five years ago my mother held his withered red apple in her hands as he lay suspended between life and death until she and my father said enough is enough and chose to take him off the machines and finish what my brother had begun. I was listening to the radio, a classical music station, mostly Mendelssohn in his semi-serene phase, and I could almost trick myself into thinking nothing had changed about the circumstances of the car or the person who once drove it; if I focused on the road and the traffic lights and the houses and the people and the trees, I could almost ignore its transformation from a perfectly functioning car into a deathmobile.

11

On my way to the hospital, I began to feel as if I might pass out from hunger, so I stopped at a brick-walled café next to a beauty salon. The Chocolate Goose was where I had my first part-time job, which involved sweeping the kitchen and greeting people at a counter where I was expected to sing joyfully and dance in place while scooping ice cream and sorbet. When I entered The Chocolate Goose and smelled the sugar, so sweet and sickly I could feel it slicking across my teeth and covering them in a sugar film, goose bumps pimpled my forearms and I shivered even though it was unseasonably hot out for the end of September. Suddenly I pictured the woman who hired me when I was fifteen and paid me in cash, under the table. She was strong, wiry, unpredictable like a goat, and back then she could've killed me if she wanted to, she could've lifted me up and dumped me into one of her vats of melted chocolate. Her arms were huge from stirring the chocolate with a wooden paddle the size of an oar. She refused to use contemporary chocolate-making equipment and techniques, as she was committed to the old-world principles, like a chocolate-making elf straight out of a children's book.

Now there she was, standing behind the counter as if she had never left. And perhaps she hadn't, perhaps she had refused to retire, or maybe she'd retired, gotten bored, and come back. Perhaps we had that in common, we couldn't stay away from the past, it kept calling out to us, requesting our presence, *Hello, is Dan Moran there? It's the past, I need to speak with you, it's pretty urgent.* She was a shrunken, ageless crone with bright white hair pulled back into a tight bun, almost sculptural, and hairy moles dotting her cheeks and pointed chin. Her dark brown eyes were narrow and hooded, like those of an evil bird from a novel, I don't even know which novel, exactly, but one of them. She wouldn't remember me, I predicted. I went up to the counter to order a cup of coffee, my vocal cords straining, my arms folded across my chest, now flat from top surgery.

Oh my Lord, she said. You're the last person I expected to see.

I heard a soothing piano album, which surprised me because she never once allowed us to listen to music while we worked, even though we were expected to sing and dance, but only to the music in our heads.

Matthias Moran, she said. It's been so long. I'm so happy to see you. What has it been, more than twenty years?

Instead of deadnaming me, she had called me by my middle brother's name. Instead of meek and mild ______ Moran, she saw Matthias Moran, Netflix content creator, and as I stood on the other side of the counter where I once worked, singing and dancing at a frenzied, joyful pitch, I was now ushered into a new identity and would have to deadname myself in order to correct her. Sometimes it's easier to go along with whatever a person believes, even if it's wrong, it's easier not to put up a fight to alter their perception. I had no idea why or how she remembered my brother Matthias Moran. Had he worked here, too?

She asked me what I was doing.

I lied and said I was on a walk.

I didn't say anything about the hospital or 212 Alexander Lane or the women who had been orbiting around my youngest brother before he died.

It was a good day for a walk, I said.

I ordered a coffee. I got out my money. She rang me up and said she looked forward to seeing me again soon.

I was startled.

Soon? I said. What do you mean by that?

She said my parents had invited her to my youngest brother's memorial dinner. Not only had she been invited, she said she was incredibly honored to provide ice cream and other assorted sweets for the memorial dinner, including a special eighty-five percent dark chocolate dipping fountain. She said symmetry can be beautiful. She had provided dessert for the small gathering after my youngest brother's funeral; five years later, she would provide dessert for his memorial.

During difficult times, that's what we turn to. We'll always have ice cream and chocolate fountains, she said in a deeply philosophical way.

From the counter, I could see back into the kitchen, I could see the industrial-size sink where I had spent countless hours after school with my head down, using the rough side of the sponge to burnish its contours until it gleamed. One afternoon while I was sweeping the white linoleum, this crone had approached me from behind, out of nowhere, and hissed into my ear, *Honey, that's not how you do it.* She claimed I didn't know how to handle the broom properly. When I was fifteen years old, The Chocolate Goose woman put her arms around me and showed me how to grip the broom handle with her liver-spotted hands. This demonstration took far longer than I would've wished, as she insisted we sweep up each square inch of the linoleum together; I was overcome with anxiety, wondering why she was so insistent on this broom-handling lesson, why does she think I do not know how to sweep when I've been sweeping my entire life, each Saturday morning I've swept the concrete floor of my parents' garage for fifty cents, does she think I'm stupid? I never told my parents about it, one of many things I kept from them; it had been more than twenty years since she grabbed me from behind with force, causing a trickle of urine to run down my leg. I couldn't believe the woman, The Chocolate Goose woman, who put her arms around me in an inhuman, animal-like fashion when I was fifteen and made me pee in my pants, had been invited to my youngest brother's memorial dinner.

But now I needed her.

I would have to interrogate her about what she had seen at my brother's funeral five years ago. Had she observed a woman who covered her face with her hands? Had she laid eyes on the woman who might have been my brother's girlfriend? Did she sense how troubled she was, the one who hid her face at the funeral? The Chocolate Goose woman must have seen things, I thought, it was always the ones working quietly behind the scenes who noticed and observed everything!! At some point I would need to tell my parents what had happened with The Chocolate Goose woman many years ago, I would need to try to persuade them to fire her, but I knew my parents would never believe me, they would never imagine she could be capable of a thing like that, to come up behind my fifteen-year-old self noiselessly and astonish me with her arms and her relentless broom-handling demonstration. It wasn't possible for her to do something like that. Not someone so small and so old and so good at making chocolate. No, they would never believe such a story. And The Chocolate Goose woman had paid me under the table, which was part of her plan, she could deny I had ever worked for her, there was no proof I had ever worked there, there wasn't a paper trail. But wait, there was once that stack of pamphlets on the counter for catering orders, I remembered. And the pamphlet had a picture of the kitchen with its silver pots and pans and vats of chocolate in liquid form, glossy and shining, vaguely sexual. And in one tiny picture, about the size of a stamp, the back of my head bent over the sink. It was proof I had worked at The Chocolate Goose. No one had asked me if they could take my picture, my least favorite form of picture. It was a picture of the back of my head, my formerly long coarse black hair hanging down past my shoulders. My big black curtain of hair. A picture of just the back of my head. But that could have been anyone's head, I reflected. There was no proof it was *my particular head.* My Korean adoptee head.

Dazed, I drank the coffee she gave me.

How is ______ doing? The Chocolate Goose woman said. I haven't seen your sister in years.

My posture stiffened at the sound of my deadname. Even the word itself, *deadname*, seemed dramatic and juvenile.

When I had worked at The Chocolate Goose, small talk with customers had been discouraged for the sake of efficiency. It must be a late-morning lull, I thought. And I hadn't expected this, I wasn't prepared at all to speak on behalf of my deadname with The Chocolate Goose woman. I took a sip of coffee and I brushed a piece of lint off my shirt while The Chocolate Goose woman wiped down the counter with a pale blue rag. Her rag was going in circles and circles. I told her I believed my sister was doing very well. She asked if she would see my sister at the memorial dinner.

It's been so many years since I've seen her, she added. I don't remember seeing her at the funeral, either.

I looked out the window of The Chocolate Goose and I saw my youngest brother's Honda Accord rumble down a pockmarked road until one of its tires became flattish.

Did your sister go to your brother's funeral? she said.

Of course she did, I lied. I have to ask, do you remember seeing a woman at the funeral who covered her face with her hands?

I'll have to think about that, she said. It's possible.

What did she look like? I said. What was her name?

It's been so many years. So many funerals.

I tried to hide my disappointment at the dead end.

Does your sister have a family of her own now? The Chocolate Goose woman asked.

I pretended not to hear her.

I don't know if you'll see her, I said, my sister might have other plans.

She was rather socially awkward, said The Chocolate Goose woman. But the youngest was the most awkward. You were the normal one.

It was strange to talk about Matthias, myself, and my youngest brother in this way, with such detachment. Part of me took pleasure in my disguise, my new identity, however fleeting. *You were the normal one*, I repeated to no one. *You were the normal one.* Rather than make self-improvements or go to therapy, perhaps it's easier to dissociate from reality, to simply detach from it, to break off and imagine oneself as an entirely new character, however repellent, off-putting, grotesque, unlikable, unhinged, etc. Perhaps this is how you change.

I left The Chocolate Goose woman and went around the tree-shaded side of the brick building where the green dumpster was. To catch my breath. Where I used to lean against the brick wall and smoke my secret cigarettes in peace. Where I used to dabble in marijuana and mushrooms. Where I used to hum songs by Fiona Apple and Sheryl Crow. Where I used to fantasize about making my escape. Where I used to interview myself about my plans to make my escape. Interviewer: How long will it take you to escape, and where will you escape to? As I looked at the green dumpster, sun glinting through the oaks, I remembered many years ago on a fifteen-minute break from The Chocolate Goose I had launched myself into its cavernous dimensions. An hour later, a maintenance man came to my rescue and helped me out.

12

When I arrived at the Ferrari Wing I texted Aunt Sue to see where everyone was. While I waited to hear from her, I poured myself a cup of coffee from a barrel-size plastic carafe and picked at a lemon Danish left on a buffet table. There were six rows of folding chairs and a small stage with four microphones flanked by two potted plants with tender yellow leaves on the far right and left. Through the openings of the coffee-stained, cream-colored vertical blinds, I could make out a wooden walkway that cut through the woods. I watched a nurse push an old man in a wheelchair, his legs covered with a blanket. She stopped occasionally to point something out to him, a bird or a tree.

I sat down in a chair, crossed my legs, and checked my phone. I was surprised not to receive an immediate response from Aunt Sue. I couldn't imagine they would've begun the special occasion without me, oldest brother of the deceased. I wondered where Matthias was. Little did he know, less than an hour ago, I had assumed his identity perfectly, I had inhabited his aura and appearance as if I were a Method actor, even though I preferred the more naturalistic performances, the effortless ones, the ones that seemed as if a person, a life, were simply being documented and accounted for.

A woman around my age or younger emerged from the depths of the hospital. Pushing a gray plastic cart, she seemed surprised by my presence but didn't say a word. She parked the cart, opened the blinds all the way, then began to clear the plastic carafes and plates of pastries from the buffet table. I took out the threatening smiley face letter.

Did you forget something? the letter writer asked.

I was mapping the route from the hospital to 212 Alexander Lane when my phone vibrated in my pocket. I knew it was Aunt Sue responding to my text, but I hoped it might be my youngest brother's high school calling to accept my proposal for a paid reading or talk.

You must give a reading at your youngest brother's high school, I told myself, no matter what. You must insist upon giving a reading at his high school.

I was disappointed to see the text was from a troubled youth demanding a workshop extension.

Excuse me, said the woman with the cart, can I help you with something?

I looked around and asked her where everyone was.

She said the quartet had already gone home, the special event was over.

The quartet? I said. What kind of quartet?

The Ferrari Wing hosts private events with music in the morning, she said.

It's over?

About thirty minutes ago.

Embarrassed, I got up from the folding chair and picked through the stack of papers at the end of the buffet table. The papers appeared to be an invitation to something. Each one had my brother's name on it, his birthday, and the day he died.

September 28, 2013. For some reason it did not specify the manner of his death.

What was more interesting to me was the small black-and-white photo of him smiling in a dull, dissociated way. An uncertain, insincere smile. He's wearing a polo shirt with a tiny crab logo, and there's a faint mustache underneath his nose, a shadow stealing across his face. I used to give him shit for the mustache, I said to myself, and now I'm paying the price with my own shitty mustache. The photo appeared to be from young adulthood, around the time he had been at the apex of his pathological-lying powers, the LeBron James of lying. The photo was nothing like the one of him playing a detective. When I looked up, I noticed the woman with the cart staring at me longer than appropriate. She lingered near the buffet table, as if she had something on her mind.

By any chance, she said, did you used to work at the mall?

It's surprising when a stranger asks a question, I thought. Whenever a stranger breaks the silence to ask a question, my stomach drops. Of course I once worked at the mall, like everyone who grows up in the suburbs of Milwaukee, but that was more than twenty years ago. And I had a different name, appearance, gender, etc.

It's just, I've seen you before, she said. Did you work at Abercrombie and Fitch?

A wave of revulsion passed through me. I couldn't believe this would be the second person of the day to mistake me for my middle brother Matthias Moran. I had transitioned to be perceived as a man, but not as my middle brother. I hadn't foreseen this possibility, although I should've known better. There are only so many Asians in Milwaukee, I said to myself, and the non-Asians can't tell us apart; they see one Asian man and there are at least twenty Asian men behind him, prepared to take his place without suffering any consequences. I didn't want to explain to the woman that it was my middle brother Matthias who once worked at Abercrombie & Fitch, whereas I had worked at the nature and incense store.

I am not the person you think I am, I could have said to her.

Yeah, I said, I used to work at Abercrombie.

She said her name was Nina and that she had worked in the food court.

I think I used to give you free pretzels on your break, she said.

The way she said this while smiling shyly seemed to hint at something else, but I wasn't sure what. I was never interested in getting to know Matthias's friends or associates. I suddenly remembered a different woman, a Korean woman, from what must have been many years ago. He'd brought her home for the only Christmas I spent with my family as a fully independent adult, and my respect for him increased by about five percent based on the woman's appearance. She was in her late thirties, early forties, but looked older because of her long white hair, which she wore as a single braid. She was vocal about why she refused to dye it. Some kind of social protest. When my mother made suggestive comments alluding to the nature of their relationship, the woman with the white braid made it clear to everyone that she was not Matthias's girlfriend, their socializing was platonic. What was the woman with the white braid's name? Maria-Louise? Suzanne? Collette? Although I never trusted people who claimed they were bad with names and faces, I might've been one of them myself.

And your name is Matthias, right? the woman with the cart said presently.

That's right. I blinked and smiled.

Matthias always smiled no matter what was happening around him. He smiled through the Christmas we hosted the woman with the white braid. He smiled when my mother came down with food poisoning and had to retire to her bedroom for the remainder of the holiday. I remembered the woman with the white braid ransacking the kitchen cabinets as my youngest brother and I watched in astonishment. She heroically baked several pies, and when she presented them to everyone, Matthias was smiling. He would've smiled all through my youngest brother's funeral if he had attended it, and now he would smile through the memorial dinner.

Nina sat down in the folding chair in front of me and turned around.

I've been to your parents' house before, she said. It's nice.

I looked out the window again and shuddered. The woman pushing the old man in the wheelchair was bent over on the walkway; it appeared she was taking a picture of a plant on her phone.

The last time I was there, you and your sister were yelling at each other, Nina said. One of your friends threw a basketball at the back of her head.

My older sister is a very strange woman, I said lightly.

I began to savor talking in third-person past tense about

who I once was, as if my previous form were an entirely new, separate character whom I could manipulate however I wanted and place in various scenarios like a role-playing game avatar.

My older sister has had a troubled life, I went on. She has had so many difficulties, I wouldn't know where to begin. She's always been a lost woman. But what about my youngest brother? What do you remember about him?

Who?

My youngest brother. A short Asian man. Plain, apologetic.

What did he look like, exactly? she said.

That's him!! I blurted out as I pointed to the stack of papers.

She went to the buffet, picked one up, and examined it.

Oh, she said.

She returned the piece of paper to the stack.

I'm sorry for your loss.

Well, do you remember him?

I think so, she said. But it was a long time ago.

Unlike my mother, Nina would not divulge easily. I would need to draw information out of Nina even if it meant I had to pretend to be my middle brother Matthias. I tried to imagine what he would do if he were interacting with a woman around his age.

If you'd like to get a drink with me later, I said, I'd love to catch up with you.

Nina looked at a coffee stain on the floor. Out of nowhere, I felt a fleeting sense of discomfort, as if I had trespassed in some way, even though I had not trespassed as myself but as my brother Matthias, who loved to trespass, who never stopped trespassing. It was interesting to trespass as him, somehow it was easier, and this reflection made me think about my so-called masculinity. It was so much easier to be inappropriate as a man in the Midwest; it was expected.

We're not supposed to go out with people we meet at the hospital, Nina said. But since you're an old friend, what's your number?

I gave it to her even though my stomach lurched at the way she said *old friend*. Had she caught on to me? Had she figured out I was pretending to be my middle brother Matthias?

My phone vibrated.

hey matthias :)

It was Nina with the second smiley face of the day. Was there a thread of connection? Before I could pursue this line of inquiry, I heard someone banging on the floor-to-ceiling windows. The caregiver of the old man in the wheelchair pressed her face against the glass. She was shouting God knows what at us. Behind her, I could see the old man flat on the ground. His leg shuddered then stilled. Two men appeared out of nowhere and wheeled a stretcher down the walkway. The body was dying or dead, someone's father, grandfather, *a royal patriarch of a man*, and only then, as Nina hurried off, leaving me alone, did I wonder about Aunt Sue and the rest of my family and what had transpired in the Ferrari Wing that morning or, more precisely, what it had to do with my youngest brother.

13

In the concrete maze of the hospital's parking structure, I walked up and down the aisles looking for my youngest brother's car. I hurried in one direction, then changed my mind due to some kind of directional intuition and set off in another. With mounting disorientation I thought of W. G. Sebald lost in his maze of dark green hedges, and how it could be said that the hedges' contours, when viewed from above, resembled the cross-section of his brain. I paced the aisles and swerved from oncoming cars. I must've spent thirty minutes wandering the parking structure, searching.

My phone was silent; there was no reception. All the cars looked the same and blurred together. I caught myself searching for a maroon car, a car from my college days in Iowa, but I was no longer in possession of the maroon car, technically it was my father who had owned the maroon car, and he gave it away to one of his friends after my youngest brother died. Instead of giving away his dead son's car, he chose to give away mine. I was about to sit down on the concrete floor to take a break from searching when I spotted the black Honda Accord next to an elevator shaft.

I was watching you, man, said a security guard. I watched you pacing around. You looked like you were about to give up on life!!

I settled into the Honda Accord and glanced at the time on the dashboard. It was early afternoon. Once I had negotiated my way out of the parking structure, I pulled into a valet lot. Idling, I glanced at my phone, which was open to a map directing me from my current location to 212 Alexander Lane. I had not received texts from Aunt Sue or anyone. I called my youngest brother's high school. Someone answered on the second ring.

This the office of Pope Pius High School, a woman's voice said.

I introduced myself as Dan Moran, the local author of *Sorry to Disrupt the Peace.* I told her if she was not familiar with me, she could look up my name on Wikipedia for more information. In general, I do not like to share the name of my book because of its attachment to my deadname; other than that, I was okay with what was inside of it.

I know you must be busy, I continued, but did you happen to have a chance to listen to my voicemail or to read any of the favorable articles I forwarded you about me and my novel?

I'm sorry, she said. I'm not sure I know what you're talking about. Are you saying you're an author? This is a high school, sir. It's not a bookstore.

I understand that, I said. My youngest brother is an alumnus of your high school. He died five years ago.

My throat was parched from the coffee I had drunk in the Ferrari Wing. I was having trouble speaking. I felt as if I had tissues in my mouth blocking my throat, the tissues my mother had used up the night before when she mentioned my youngest brother.

I'm sorry, she said.

You see, he died unexpectedly, as they say.

. . .

What I mean is he took his own life, I said. He committed suicide in his car. Five years ago. A black Honda Accord. Right outside of the hospital with the Ferrari Wing.

The tissues were in the back of my mouth again. Great big balls of wadded-up sob-soaked tissues.

I'm very sorry, sir, she said.

I'm sitting in his car right now, I added.

After a long silence, she said, I'm sorry to hear that.

I put the phone on mute so she wouldn't hear me blow my nose into my sleeve. A week after my youngest brother died, a stranger knocked at the door of my childhood home and handed me a helium balloon with a card from my roommate Julie. *I'm so sorry for your loss, I hope this balloon helps. <3 Julie <3.* The balloon was my grief balloon and it bobbed gently in the corner of my childhood bedroom for a few days, and it didn't take long for me to associate the presence of the grief balloon with my youngest brother and his habit of standing in the corner with his arms folded across his chest, nodding at various points of a social interaction to signal absolute agreement and approval. The grief balloon was now my dead brother, and when it deflated five days later, just as I was about to recover mentally and get back on my feet again and think about returning to my troubled youth in New York, to see my grief balloon withered and wrinkled flat on the carpet in the corner of my bedroom caused me to suffer another mental collapse, and instead of returning to New York, I returned to my observation post on my parents' couch in the middle of my childhood living room. Right as I was about to get back on my feet, I suffered a minor setback thanks to the presence of the grief balloon, utterly wilted, resigned, defeated, and I felt nothing as I stared at the piece of crinkled foil on the floor that had been the grief balloon, once full of promise and vitality and light, nodding, bobbing, approving, a presence just as physically animated and sensitive and attuned to the feelings of others as any human I'd ever met or encountered since.

Are you there? said the woman.

Wikipedia, I said, there are links on Wikipedia.

I'm just not sure . . . how all of this connects, sir, she said.

I cleared my throat and reiterated how I wanted to give a paid reading and talk in memory of my youngest brother, an important alumnus of the high school. I left out the part about my intention to draw out his high school friends and interrogate them about the woman at the funeral who might have been my brother's girlfriend.

I work with records and attendance, said the woman. I'm not in charge of events.

I see, perhaps you could tell the person in charge of events that a local author would like to make an appearance.

What was your brother's name?

I told her.

Can I place you on a brief hold, sir?

A song from the baroque period came on, all flashing harpsichords and jaunty flutes; it resembled the theme song of *Murder, She Wrote*, its melody alternating between total despair and cheerful emotional valences, which was, I now decided, what almost all classical music sounded like.

Hello? This is Millie Baker. How can I help you?

Millie Baker's voice was higher-pitched and more energetic than the previous person's. I reintroduced myself. After the conversation with the woman from records and attendance, I was now well rehearsed in how to explain the situation regarding my youngest brother and my reading. This time, to prevent the balled-up-tissue feeling in my mouth, I avoided talking about the circumstances of my youngest brother's death. I kept the details vague and utilized the phrase *unexpected death in the family*. I said nothing about the deathmobile. I didn't even tell her I was sitting in his car. I lied and said I was calling from my spacious home office. I might have said I was about to swivel around in my Herman Miller leather chair and look out the window.

Sorry, what? Millie Baker said. Home office something?

It's not important, I said. I'm wondering if we can work out the dates for my reading at your high school for this fall semester. As soon as possible would be best for me—

Millie Baker interrupted and said she was the director of alumni relations. Before I could get another word in, she explained that she had talked to the events coordinator about my proposal, and although the school's schedule was completely full in terms of booking events, she would be more than happy to help me set up a recurring donation in honor of my youngest brother's death.

We always make sure to take special care of our alumni, she said. Does a memorial bench with a very unique engraving or a small but tasteful plaque appeal to you?

. . .

We also have some options for people with smaller budgets, she added.

She told me about the things people had engraved on their memorial plaques and benches, such as BIGDADDY R.I.P. I couldn't help but picture a bench with my youngest brother's name on it in some dark corridor of the high school where teenagers sat down and tried to do drugs. As she described the unique engravings of the memorial plaques and benches, I became convinced she was making a mockery of me.

I would prefer to do the reading, I said. I'll do it for free.

I'm sorry, sir, but we schedule events far in advance. We'll be booking next year's events in a month or so. You're welcome to circle back then. In the meantime, I'd love to get you connected with our alumni relations office. What's your most recent mailing address?

I don't have one, I said.

Oh, I thought you said you had a home office. I'm sorry I misunderstood. Do you have a second so I can get some updated contact information from you?

Of course I don't have time to connect with the alumni relations office, I thought. I should be driving home to work on my psychological thriller. I should be conducting an investigation of 212 Alexander Lane. Now that I had turned off the Do Not Disturb setting, I should write back to my troubled youth. To make up for the fact that I never attended my uncle's funeral, I should catch up with Aunt Sue after all these years. Her lifelong companion, a morning jogger, was struck by a blue Tacoma—and how had she filled her days since his death?

What had I been doing with myself?

Had I overlooked something?

Sir, do you have a moment to give me your email address so I can add it to our alumni and friends network?

I'm sorry, Millie, I don't have a moment, I said, and I hung up.

14

I had become obsessed with the idea of giving a reading at the high school, certain it would solve my remaining questions about my youngest brother and the unexplained mysteries surrounding his life and death, and although I was disappointed with my conversation with Millie Baker, I wasn't discouraged.

I sat in my brother's car. On my phone I looked up Pope Pius High School's upcoming events page. Tomorrow evening there would be a reading by a local poet, a person named Matilda Pierre. I glanced at her website; she had published numerous poetry collections focused on the healing powers of nature, prayer, and walking. I emailed Matilda Pierre to explain my situation and to ask her if I would be welcome to join her as a reader that night. Although I was not viewed as a spirituality writer, I thought the themes of my work, dysfunctional families, suicide, transnational adoption, etc. would make a fine juxtaposition to whatever she was doing, I explained to her in my email. Nature, prayer, and walking, perhaps she was a Christian version of W. G. Sebald. Satisfied with the composition of my email, I pressed send. I noticed I had no messages or voicemails from Aunt Sue or Uncle Karl, not even one troubled youth.

The only person who wanted to talk with me, the only one who had invited me anywhere, was the one who had sent me the threatening smiley face letter.

Did you forget something?

Instead of going home, I decided to drive by 212 Alexander Lane, the apartment complex. According to my phone, I was ten minutes away. At a stoplight, I noticed an Asian man in a blue Kia Soul to the right of me, staring in my direction. Perhaps he was surprised to see another Asian driving to and fro in the suburbs of Milwaukee, since there were so few of us. I couldn't tell if his look of surprise was a friendly, convivial one or apprehensive, shaded with minor dread. He had dark hair and a face like a piece of plywood, smooth, featureless. His eyes were small dark brown pebbles like my youngest brother's. A shudder of recognition went through me, as if he were someone I had been close to. The white woman next to him said something. He turned to her, then to me. I rolled down my passenger window.

Excuse me, do I know you? I said.

The Asian man gave me a sidelong glance, then shook his head. His eyes were wide.

Was he afraid of me?

Have we met before? I shouted. What is it? Do I have a flat tire?

The Asian man, rigid in the driver's seat, kept his eyes straight ahead. Perhaps he was a self-hating Asian or perhaps he thought I was a self-hating Asian, perhaps he thought I was shouting an obscenity at him. The light changed and a car behind me honked. My brother's car jolted forward, the Asian man turned right, and I was alone.

15

At the beginning of the post-suicide phase, some people in my family thought I was laughing at death, they thought I was laughing at suicide. My relatives looked at me perched on my parents' couch in the living room, my observation post, and they thought I was laughing at death and suicide. I tried to conceal my laughter by putting my hands in front of my mouth. What kind of emotional support is that? I overheard my father's sister ask a cousin in the dining room. Sitting on the living room couch, doing nothing, observing, occasionally commenting on what I had observed, occasionally grazing on a piece of food, whatever anyone offered me, I munched steadily into oblivion, satisfied, completely bovine. And now here I was, five years later, out in the world, driving around the city of my childhood in my youngest brother's car, wind whipping through the windows. Investigating.

As I was about to turn onto Alexander Lane, five minutes from the apartment complex, I came to a stop. I glanced in my rearview mirror and happened to see the outline of two familiar-looking people in the car behind me.

It was my mother and her sister, engaged in a lively conversation, or perhaps they had heard something amusing on the radio; they didn't notice me right in front of them, their eyes were everywhere but directly ahead.

How often is that the case, I thought, we're always looking where we shouldn't be, it almost never happens that our eyes alight on the very thing we should be looking at, at exactly the right moment. It's a miracle it happens at all!! No, first my mother failed to recognize me, her son, then she failed to recognize her other son's black Honda Accord, even with his deathmobile idling right before her eyes and his 666 license plate. I switched out of the right lane and allowed my mother to pass me. Perhaps my mother might turn her head to the left and notice me, her son, in the driver's seat and wave hello, but she and her sister were laughing like little girls, oblivious to their surroundings. I opened the console of my youngest brother's car and found a pair of sunglasses, cheap aviator sunglasses with mirrored lenses from a gas station and put them on, even though the sky had become overcast. I swerved back into the right lane and now trailed behind my mother and Aunt Sue. My mother was driving slowly as if she had all the time in the world to get to her destination. Without thinking about what I was doing, without a plan, I decided to follow her.

My mother turned left on a blinking yellow light, and I raced through the intersection to keep up, normally I would've stopped, but not now, now I was a detective driving a car. As I sped through the blinking yellow light, an oncoming truck swerved away from me, the truck driver's face frozen in horror, his truck tilting, tilting at an angle suggestive of imminent tipping over, nearly occasioning an accident at the intersection. It reminded me of the time I watched a baby crawl into oncoming traffic on Coney Island Avenue in Brooklyn. And yet, by some miracle, the truck righted and passed through the intersection without killing anyone or the driver himself.

I wasn't sure what happened to the baby. I kept following my mother. After a mile down a suburban street populated by chain restaurants, she pulled into a shopping plaza, one I was familiar with from my high school years.

Instead of pulling into the shopping plaza, I parked my brother's car at the gas station across the street. As a detective, I needed to survey the scene from afar. My mother and Aunt Sue stepped out of the car and stood at the entrance of a Chinese restaurant, where they met with a middle-aged man, a woman, and a child. The five of them exchanged embraces. The man was not my father, not my cousin Fran, not my uncle; I could only assume the man was my middle brother Matthias, but it was difficult to tell from so far away. I glanced at myself in the rearview mirror. He didn't know who I was anymore, I thought. No, he never knew who I was, I clarified as I watched them go into the Chinese restaurant.

16

I felt tense about seeing Matthias, then I realized I was wearing the aviator sunglasses, which covered half of my face and would betray no emotion whatsoever. No one would recognize me especially if I smiled. I was not a smiler. I walked past the entrance of the restaurant to the opposite end of the plaza, occasionally looking into the shopwindows. There was the used bookstore where I would switch price tags and a clothing store for pregnant women. Behind the plaza was an alley. I almost tripped over the rancid contents spilling out of a black garbage bag as I fumbled my way toward a back door propped open with a brick. I entered what turned out to be the kitchen of the Chinese restaurant where an old man sat on a milk crate peeling a navel orange. There was a box fan on the floor pushing out the greasy air. I was familiar with kitchens in Chinese restaurants, since my second job, post–The Chocolate Goose, had been as a host at a restaurant called Chin's. I wondered why I was a host, never a server, I must've been too dumb to be a server. I walked into the kitchen and past the man on the crate as if I were clocking in for a shift. I gave him a downward nod. He nodded in return. There was another man at the sink, spraying food-encrusted dishes with a long hose. He said something in my direction, but I couldn't understand, so I grunted in response. I had learned grunting was an acceptable way for men to communicate. Someone had left a dirty baseball cap on the counter and I tried it on.

I could feel the dampness of the brim against my forehead. When I was certain none of my relatives or family members would recognize me, I left the kitchen, smiling. As I turned into the hallway where the bathrooms were, Aunt Sue ran directly into my chest.

Dan? she said. Is that you?

I pulled the baseball cap lower.

No, not really, I said.

Your hat says *Playboy Magazine*, she said, laughing. Do you subscribe to *Playboy*? By the way, I didn't see you at the hospital. Where have you been?

Sorry about that, I said. I've been busy.

Doing what, though? she said.

I was worried my mother or Matthias would ambush me in the hallway.

I'll explain later, I said. I've got to run.

Aunt Sue stepped aside and I sneaked into the dining room, which was thankfully dim. I spotted a stack of extra chairs in a corner. I once sat in this Chinese restaurant with a high school friend whom I've since lost touch with. My friend and I didn't have money, so we ordered hot tea, which was free, and one serving of egg rolls. We would spend hours in the booth with our egg rolls; my friend liked to eat the center of the egg roll and would leave behind shards of rice-paper wrapper all over the plate and table. Years later she drove two hours from Milwaukee to my reading in downtown Chicago. My high school friend and I had nothing to say to each other. We had known each other only during the most acutely painful phases of our lives, and even though we promised to catch up on the past twenty years, we never did. To call her to catch up after all these years would've been a grievous social blunder. In college at Iowa it had been easy for me to make friends, I had a surplus of them, whereas in high school it took me three years to make two friends, an average of fewer than one friend per year.

I hid behind the stack of chairs and looked out of my observation post at the red vinyl booths. My mother and the man, woman, and child she had greeted in the parking lot were sitting in a large U-shaped booth near the entrance. I wondered if they were expecting more people to join them. The thought came into my head that it was possible they were expecting me, but it was more interesting to observe them from my post behind the stack of chairs, undetected. A server approached the U-shaped booth, and I watched the man who I suspected was my middle brother put in an order. When he turned his head to speak, in profile, I became certain it was him. It was his youthful face, his wolfish black hair styled upward and out, his clear plastic-framed round glasses. Having observed my middle brother Matthias sitting in the booth from my observation post behind the stack of chairs, I felt thoroughly exhausted and slightly antisocial.

I might see Michael in Chicago tonight, I heard him say.

Matthias said his filmmaker friend Michael was making a documentary about Korean adoptees and wanted to interview him. He described for my mother some of Michael's footage and how all the adoption stories were similar, abandonment in public places without any identifying information, a baby in booties left on a doorstep, a DOB on a piece of paper pinned to a coat, but no other clues, nothing.

But aren't you happy we adopted you? she said.

Yeah, Mom, he said. I'm happy you adopted me.

My mother changed the subject and asked if he'd seen me since he got in.

Why isn't she here with us? he said. What is she doing?

And I thought I heard my mother say, She's been struggling with some issues, as you know, for many years.

Several times throughout their conversation I thought I should stand up and walk toward them and exclaim, WHAT THE FUCK DID YOU SAY ABOUT ME?, but instead of standing up and exclaiming, I had no choice but to remain in my position behind the chairs.

No, I don't know, said Matthias. I don't talk with her.

Why not?

She doesn't like me. She never did. Didn't you know that?

But she's your big sister, you'll always have a special bond.

We're not like you and your sisters. We're not close.

Why not, though?

For one thing, I don't trust her. She's never said anything nice about our family especially my brother. Besides, if she had really cared about him, if she had liked him, she would've been there for him. Instead she pretends she liked him, as if the two of them were close, and she's exploited the situation for her own personal gain. Out of all of us, hasn't she been the one to gain the most out of what happened?

I guess I haven't thought about it that way, said my mother.

She took my brother's suicide and wrote a book about it. I never read his suicide letter, out of respect for him. She did the opposite. She read his suicide letter, what should've remained private, and made it public. Now everyone knows what he said before he died.

Even from across the restaurant, I could tell he was about to start crying.

I don't know what she wrote about, said my mother. I didn't read her book.

We're not family to her, said my middle brother Matthias, we're not her relatives, we're her resources. Uncle Karl told me she has questions. About what happened to him. She won't let it go. What difference does it make?

What could she possibly need to know about him now? my mother asked. After all this time?

And that's what it sounded like they said, although I couldn't be certain, perhaps halfway through I stopped listening as closely as I could have, perhaps I tuned out halfway through because at times it can be an emotional drain to listen to a person's complaints, especially an immediate family member's; besides, there was something at my foot that required my utmost attention while they were speaking. A small brownish ladybug crawled across the carpet very slowly, a Sebaldian creature moving soundlessly as if it were half dead or in an anesthetized nocturnal trance, and I imagined, as Sebald would, what an ordeal it must be to cross the carpet's terrain, the scale of which must be similar to a human making their way across a town, city, country, continent, the slightest warp or fold in the carpet akin to a mountain peak in

China or Nepal. It became increasingly difficult to hear what Matthias and my mother were discussing from across the restaurant with the din of the servers who clanked steaming platters of food on the tables and shouted at one another incomprehensible phrases such as *fresh new fork now*, but that was what I had heard when occasionally the clatter would subside from where I was positioned, crouched behind the stack of chairs. Perhaps Matthias and my mother had used the pronoun *he*, I reflected, not *she*. There was no way for me to know for sure, it was far too late for me to come out from behind the stack of chairs, approach them, and inquire.

The U-shaped booth was silent after my middle brother's rant, and I wondered if what he had said was part of his speech, the speech he had prepared for my youngest brother's memorial. Was he rehearsing his speech right in front of them? I wondered. I could picture him walking up to a podium, tapping the microphone. *If she had really cared about him, if she had liked him, she would've been there for him.*

I need to write a rebuttal, I said to myself.

A rebuttal to my brother Matthias's speech.

From behind the stack of chairs, I could make out the long hair of a woman seated next to my middle brother; she was nodding in agreement to whatever Matthias said. It was his wife, the mother of his child, nodding in a maternal way. And it struck me I hadn't heard Matthias's voice in five years, since that day we talked on the phone and laughed at our dead brother. I couldn't remember the last time I had heard his voice in person. Perhaps it was the Christmas he brought home the woman with the white braid, but I couldn't be sure.

Instead of talking to Matthias, the one who my family members believed had all the answers, I remained at my observation post. For years I had avoided looking at Matthias's face, his Korean adoptee face, like mine but not at all, and it hadn't occurred to me that he might have been waiting for me all this time at the Chinese restaurant, perhaps he had anticipated my arrival as much as I had dreaded seeing him and stalled it, he might have nervously glanced at the entrance to see if I would show up, each time the door jingled open, his stomach dropped in expectation, even if he didn't know who I was now, when he looked at me, he would be reminded of *who he was* and the things he had done; he must've expected me to make an appearance at the Chinese restaurant, even though I had not been directly invited by anyone, even though I was hardly invited anywhere and was forced to insinuate my way into invitations to events, dinners, parties, readings, classrooms, workshops, lectures, etc.

I watched Aunt Sue come out of the dim hallway and return to the U-shaped booth. She whispered to my mother, who sat up straight and looked around, scanning the room, it was likely she hoped to spot me and invite me over, but it was too late for any of that, I was already on my way out.

17

Another abandoned writing project of mine was titled *Afternoon Hours of a Hermit*, because the afternoon was a time of day I disliked, a time I preferred to spend asleep if I wasn't teaching or responding to emails from my troubled youth at the private arts college. *Afternoon Hours of a Hermit* was a collection of nap dreams I recorded on my phone. May 4, 3:42 p.m.: *I look in the mirror and instead of a face I see a featureless beige square. I try to smile but the beige square will not move. I realize my life has changed in an irrevocable manner.* When I emailed *Afternoon Hours of a Hermit* to Thomas Bernhard, my mentor, he didn't have anything to say about it. When I emailed *Afternoon Hours of a Hermit* to a few writer friends, they didn't have anything to say, either. When I read from *Afternoon Hours of a Hermit* out loud in front of my troubled youth during a writing workshop, I asked them, post-reading, if they had any comments or questions for me. No, nothing. I never knew what to do with myself in the afternoon besides sleeping or teaching, so it was a pleasure to drive the car with a specific destination in mind.

I suggest you come to this address: 212 Alexander Lane.

I pictured the blurred long-haired ghost figure I had seen earlier that morning, frozen for all eternity in Google Maps, stepping out of her vehicle in the parking lot. As I ruminated, I discovered that the longer I sat in the driver's seat, the seat where my youngest brother decided to die, the longer I sat there and stared at the road in front of me, the faster a dark gray thread began to unspool until my thoughts eventually took on a deathward valence. And I remembered that, a couple of years ago, I had done a favor for a writer friend in Manhattan in exchange for the use of his car for a week, and as soon as I procured his car, a white Saab, I drove from my studio apartment in Manhattan to Brooklyn across the Manhattan Bridge, sometimes I would drive with a purpose, to teach my troubled youth at the private arts college, other times I would drive simply for the satisfaction of it, for the sense of traveling somewhere at a high speed.

Driving in the city could be an aesthetically pleasing experience especially around five or six in the morning without traffic, in the darkness, when I would cross the bridge and look over the side of the Manhattan Bridge and realize how easy, how simple, it would be to jerk the steering wheel as hard as I could to the right and swerve my writer friend's white Saab into the edgeless, curving void below. What would it take to really let go and swerve off the side of the bridge? What state of mind would I need to inhabit? Around the time I drove across the Manhattan Bridge, the question of suicide had been on my mind, as a different writer friend, not the Saab owner, had told me she was writing a book about a young woman living in San Francisco who can't decide if she wants to kill herself. A year after she told me on the phone she wanted to write a book about a woman who can't decide if she wants to kill herself, my writer friend died, and although her death wasn't officially labeled a suicide, I was ninety percent certain it was. I did not know her family members, so I couldn't ask them what had happened, and when I asked our mutual friends, a few said they too believed she had killed herself, but no one knew how; one person said they thought it was an accident, not a suicide, since our friend had seemed excited about her future plans, she had decided she wanted to go back to school to get a degree in social work to help troubled people. All I know is when I had set up a reading for my book, she asked me if she could read, too, and at the time I thought it was odd that she was asking to join my reading without an invitation, as I had already set up the reading with a few other writer friends, but it was just like my writer friend to seize the opportunity by the reins and invite herself to join my reading. She was not an easy person to get along with, she once told a famous writer how much she despised him during the Q&A portion of his reading, her behavior was unpredictable, her mascara ran down her cheeks in black lines, the ice cubes in her iced latte were all melted and she would thrust her lukewarm melting iced latte at me and ask if I wanted a sip, go on, take a sip, drink it, ______, I don't want it anymore, she could be demanding and abrasive and messy when she wasn't in her manic storytelling mode, and I didn't respond to her request to join my reading, I didn't say anything to her about joining my reading, I said nothing, and that was the last time I heard from her, or perhaps the very last time was the text she sent me to ask what I was doing because it was her birthday, she said she was alone in the city and she hated being alone but she was always alone especially on her birthday even though she had a little dog and a roommate, it's possible I, too, was alone although I was never really alone because I had a roommate, my roommate Julie, and that's likely the very last message I have from her. It didn't stand out to me as much as the other message about her joining my reading, perhaps because her rudeness stood out to me more than her loneliness, although her loneliness was sadder, her rudeness was more interesting, at times it could be intoxicating to be around, and I didn't respond to the birthday text, either, and my nonresponses, I reflected, the nonresponses I had thought about but never articulated, hovered in the air to this day and troubled me whenever I saw her book displayed prominently at a bookstore or a troubled youth mentioned having admired it.

According to the map, I was a mile away from 212 Alexander Lane, and I was thinking about how my dead writer friend did not have a funeral, or at least she did not have a funeral that I was personally invited to. Perhaps what really bothered me was that my friend was dead for two months before her rumored suicide became publicly known to her writer friends and teachers. During those two months, on occasion I had looked at her texts and an inner voice had told me I should write back to her, I kept thinking I should see how she was doing even though I wondered if it was too late, too late to respond to an old text, far too late from either a social-etiquette perspective or a logistical one because by that point it was no longer her birthday. Of course, at that point, the point of having been far too late, she was already dead and had been for two months, but I didn't know, how was I to know? For those two months I had believed she was alive, living, breathing, writing, working, walking her little dog in the East Village, etc., until I saw the announcement on social media and then I came to know what I didn't want to know, that my writer friend was dead.

18

A bright yellow banner fluttered in the wind outside the leasing office at 212 Alexander Lane: Normandy Village Apartments, first month's rent free. There was a light autumnal drizzle, reminding me of those late afternoons from childhood when I had finished my homework and there was nothing else to do. I did not see any long-haired figures exiting their cars in the parking lot, which meandered around clusters of shabby, dark brown apartments. The apartment complex was larger, more sprawling than the image I had examined on Google Maps.

I drove past brown dumpsters crammed with furniture and boxes; someone had moved out or had been evicted. Boxes upon boxes. From the driver's seat, I could see into one of the ground-level apartments. The face of a black dog panted at me. It had small, round cocoa-colored eyes. The threatening smiley face letter did not specify a particular unit number. An abundance of invasive trees and shrubs obscured the sliding glass doors and balconies. It would be easy for someone to hide behind them and observe whatever tedious domestic dramas unfolded inside.

From the driver's seat, I didn't observe any activity in the units, not even the soft blue gleam of a television or a computer. It was the middle of the day, and only one or two units had their windows cracked open hardly an inch; I could hear a person practicing the piano, a plaintive fugue by Mendelssohn. My youngest brother adored all the towering piano talents. Mendelssohn, Bach, Tori Amos.

I made my way back to the leasing office. A detective would go in and talk to people, I thought. I stepped out of the car. Inside, a middle-aged woman in a lilac blouse stood behind the counter. I could see she was playing a game on her phone; we both became mesmerized by the jewels clicking into place, then exploding on her screen. I introduced myself as a private investigator and said I needed to speak with a person who lived in the Normandy Village Apartments. I wasn't sure what had come over me, why I had spoken with so much authority. Without looking up, the woman behind the counter asked me whom I needed to speak to.

I'm not sure, I said. But your tenant sent me this.

I slid the letter across the counter. The woman glanced at it.

Do you know who at Normandy Village Apartments would have written a letter like this? I said.

Do you have a unit number? she said.

Not specified, I said.

It could be from anyone, then. She shrugged.

It was obvious to me she wanted to end the conversation.

Is there a particular tenant who seems mentally and emotionally capable of writing and mailing something like this? I asked.

I pointed at the smiley face.

This looks threatening, doesn't it? I said.

The woman looked up at me for the first time.

Did you used to live here?

No.

She was looking at me.

Are you sure? You never lived here?

I live and work in New York.

Really?

But I might be interested in moving here, I said without thinking.

Information's over there, she said.

She nodded at a metal rack attached to the wall with several brochures. I helped myself to one and put it in my pocket.

It's against the law to discuss a specific tenant unless there's a signed authorization or a warrant for the person's arrest, she said. But you already know that, right?

. . .

Because you're an investigator, she said.

A metaphysical one, I thought but did not say, and with some embarrassment, I turned and stared out the window at the stark gray flatness of the parking lot.

I guess I'll have to come back with an authorization, then, I said.

I tried to say it in a threatening manner so she knew I was serious. I wondered how I would obtain an authorization, considering I didn't know who the letter writer was. Outside the window I noticed the Asian man from the intersection getting out of his blue Kia Soul. What was he doing here? Had he followed me? I felt a wave of vertigo and gripped the brochure rack to steady myself. He had parked next to my youngest brother's car. I heard footsteps, then a white envelope dropped to the floor from the mail slot. It looked exactly like the white envelope with the threatening smiley face.

As the woman came out from behind the counter to collect it, I remained at the window. I waited until the man had walked a good distance away from the leasing office then I thanked the woman for the brochure and left. I stopped at the Honda Accord to grab my sunglasses. The fine drizzle had become moderate, enough to obscure what was around me.

Underneath a dim, colorless sky, I put on my sunglasses and followed the Asian man up the walkway. A woman in yoga wear emerged from one of the brown buildings and gave him a wide berth. She did a double take when she noticed me trailing behind him; even though he and I looked nothing alike, to the woman, it didn't matter, he and I had the same face. It was possible she had never seen two Asians in the same place at the same time.

I followed him past some overturned deck chairs and a swimming pool covered with a beige tarp. I wondered if he had something to do with the threatening smiley face letter. *But I feel as if I know you very well.* The letter writer had claimed to know how much I would like the answers to my unsettling and difficult circumstances. *We are closer than you think.* We had traveled about a quarter of a mile across the complex when suddenly, without warning, he broke into a sprint. He cut across the yellowing grass and fled up some concrete steps into an entrance covered by a light brown awning spotted with rust. I wondered if the man was running from me or if he was running because of the rain. I stood underneath the awning and tried to open the entrance, but it was locked. My clothes were getting soaked.

I wandered along the exterior walkway, my shoes squishing, until I saw a light come on in one of the first-floor units. The Asian man appeared in the window and cracked it open. A woman entered the room, the white woman I had seen in the passenger seat of his car. She turned her attention to something waist-high. Based on the woman's movements, it seemed she was chopping an onion.

Underneath the windowsill was a large invasive shrub. I pushed past its branches and thorns and pointy leaves as if looking for an object I had dropped, then I ducked down so no one would see what I was doing. I could hear the man say things like *peculiar situation* and *odd coincidence.* The smell of fried onions and cumin wafted out, and parts of their conversation became clear.

It was like seeing a ghost, he said, I swear it's him.

Because of the blandness of the Midwestern palate, I realized I had not tasted cumin until I went to college. My entire childhood, I had no idea what it was.

But it can't be him, of course, he went on. That would make no sense. Unless . . .

I couldn't make out exactly what the woman was saying. I thought I heard her say, It's okay, Zachary. You're just imagining things. It's that time of year, you know. The end of September. It's a sad time for all of us.

19

I left the Normandy Village Apartments with an unsettled feeling in the pit of my stomach. An Asian man named Zachary talked with his girlfriend or wife while they made dinner. What did any of it have to do with me or my youngest brother? *I'm just not sure . . . how all of this connects, sir.* At least the Pope Pius High School administrative assistant had called me *sir*, I reflected. I turned on the windshield wipers, and instead of wiping, they squeaked against the glass, the metronome of their squeaks lulling me into a deeply meditative state of mind.

I checked my phone. Matilda Pierre had not responded to *my overly friendly solicitation*. I sent her a reminder email with the subject line: FOLLOWING UP? Then I called the administrative office of Pope Pius High School and left a voicemail asking if it would be possible for the featured writer Matilda Pierre to contact me at her earliest convenience.

Back at my childhood home, before I could sit down and contemplate what had happened that afternoon, my cousin Fran pulled me aside in the living room and asked if we could talk privately. He motioned toward a cousin sitting in an armchair, reading a book, and another one doing a puzzle on the floor.

Not to be paranoid, he whispered, but something's been bothering me.

Does it have to do with *Leaving Las Vegas?* I said.

Before he could answer, my parents and several relatives

came in and sat down. I heard my mother and Aunt Sue discussing the quartet at the Ferrari Wing that morning and how solemn and meaningful their playing had been for everyone who had attended.

He loved Bach, didn't he, my father said.

He also liked Tori Amos, I said.

Tori who? said my mother. Was that a friend of his?

No one asked me where I had been or for my investigative insights. Instead my father asked if I had been driving the Honda Accord all day. When I nodded, he looked angry. He said I should always ask permission before using other people's belongings. *But what if the owner of the car is dead?* I wanted to ask. He went on to say it was Matthias's car now. They were giving my youngest brother's car to him. I should make sure to fill up the tank because Matthias would drive it back to Los Angeles in a few days.

It took me a moment to register what my father had said.

You're giving the car to him? I said. Why are you doing that?

. . .

Why are you giving Matthias my brother's car? I said.

No one responded and I felt lightheaded and warm. In a few days Matthias would drive my brother's black Honda Accord across the gray flatness of the Midwest into the mountains, then the desert. What had he done to deserve my brother's car? The phone rang out sharply in the kitchen, disrupting my rage, and one of my cousins went to answer it. Even in my lightheaded, nauseated state, I somehow remembered to ask my parents if they had received any strange phone calls. My father said occasionally when the phone rang and he answered, the caller didn't say anything but refused to hang up, which infuriated my father until he was left shouting, Hello? Who's there? What do you want? Why don't you say something? Speak!! Everyone sitting in the living room said they had received calls like that before. They said there was nothing one could do about those kinds of calls, even though the calls were disturbing psychologically. What does the caller want? they asked. It's what's left unsaid, what's left unspoken, that is upsetting. Your mind will fill the silence with the worst things possible.

My father said that what was highly unusual about these calls was sometimes he could hear what sounded like a woman crying.

But she never says anything, he said.

And I couldn't help but think of the late-night caller.

The woman who claimed she was looking for the sister.

20

After a quiet, uneventful spaghetti dinner with my parents, Uncle Karl, Aunt Sue, Fran, and some other cousins I had never seen before, my mother asked me to help her do the dishes. She always chose me, the once-female, to assist her in the kitchen; I would clear the table, load the dishwasher, scrub the pots and pans, dry them with a thin towel, etc., while my brothers sat in the basement, where I would eventually join them to watch television. Where I would sit on the floor with a pillow on my lap.

In the kitchen my mother was wiping the counter with an old rag I recognized from my childhood kitchen duties.

Have you heard from your brother today? my mother said.

Which brother? I said.

Matthias, of course, she said. I really think he could use your support. He says he never hears from you.

. . .

I think it's nice to stay in contact with people, my mother went on. It's nice to stay in touch with people from the past, people who have known you a long time. People need people.

Where is he, then? I said.

He's spending the night in Chicago, she said. His friend Michael is making a film about him.

But why would he need my support? I said.

I tried to hide my excitement at the possibility Matthias wasn't doing well.

Oh, I don't know.

She sighed.

He was trapped in a depression for a long time. It sounds like he's finally coming out of it.

Was he depressed because of what happened to my youngest brother or was it something else? Was it guilt over something he had done?

I think he has regrets, she said.

By any chance, I said, did you keep a list of everyone who attended my youngest brother's funeral?

Why would you need that? she said suspiciously. Are you pretending to be a detective again?

Little did she know I wasn't pretending, I was turning myself into one, fully embodied. All I needed to do was walk around and look at things, and suddenly my investigative identity, dormant for years, would be revitalized.

Why must you know who was at his funeral? she repeated. Dear God, why? What are you doing to us?

She put her hands up to her face and turned away from me. She snatched the roll of paper towels from the counter and ripped off a panel and blew her nose.

Your mother still finds some of this very upsetting, my father said as he stood in the kitchen doorframe, so I think it's best, if any other questions arise, you direct them to me.

My father asked me if I had received his note that morning.

What note? I said.

The only note I could think of was the one with the threatening smiley face. My father said he needed to discuss some important financial matters with me. I followed him into the two-story foyer, away from my mother.

I don't want to alarm you, he was saying, but we've been getting calls from a medical bill collector's office. A woman is looking for you. I told her you no longer live at this address. She asked how to get in touch with you, and I said to her, I can give you her number but otherwise I don't know. She said to me, Sir, are you saying you don't know where your own daughter is? How can that be? I said to the woman, We hardly ever hear from her, she never writes back, we haven't seen her in years. That's really sad, the woman said to me, my father said, maybe you should try to find your daughter and get her some help.

. . .

Anyway, your mother and I have been discussing how wonderful it would be if you could start handling financial matters on your own. We've always supported your artistic endeavors, even the ones that negatively impacted us, but now that you're approaching forty years old, it might be time for us to move on, to move forward.

My arm hairs stood on end when I heard my father say the phrases *financial matters*, *on your own*, and *move forward*. Behind my father's head was the wall of photos, and I was staring at my youngest brother's high school graduation portrait. I realized all my high school graduation portraits had been removed.

Who took down my pictures on the wall? I said. Was it Matthias?

My father said he himself had removed a few of the photos because they upset my mother, but the real estate agent suggested they keep some of them up until they sold the house. People like to see family photos on display, even if they're pictures of a very special, nontraditional, transracial adoptive one; it's easier for them to imagine living there and making their own memories, the real estate agent had told them.

Like this one, my father said.

It was an eight-by-eleven photo taken in a professional photography studio at the mall featuring Matthias, my youngest brother, and me. The two assigned-males-at-birth were in matching pale blue suits, whereas I had been forced into a floral-patterned dress with puffy pink sleeves. The studio had tried, in what must've been a post-production stage, to make my eyes appear more feminine by adding a thick coating of grotesque curly eyelashes, such as what would be appropriate for a cartoon female cow. The photography studio had added this peculiar enhancement to my youngest brother's eyes as well, perhaps to make his eyes appear larger, rounder, more lively. I realized now it could be said that, from my family's perspective, *the two of us had died*, both my previous form and my youngest brother.

Each photo on the wall featured at least one *now-dead person*.

My daughter was once an attractive young woman, my father said as he squinted at me.

And then I swore I heard him say, Where did she go? What happened to her?

21

There was no time to ruminate on past lives or past selves. It was time to act. I shook my father's hand and thanked him for the conversation. I said I needed to go upstairs to work on my psychological thriller. Unlike Aunt Sue, he didn't bother to ask me what it was about. As soon as I sat at my desk in my childhood bedroom, the landline rang. On the fourth ring, I got up from my desk and answered it.

Hello? I said.

Matthias, is that you?

Instead of the garbled voice from last night, this woman sounded timid but clear.

Matthias? Are you there?

No, I said, this is Dan Moran.

There was silence, so I explained my name was once something else, but now it was Dan. Miraculously the woman caught on, she said she was happy for me, then she told me her name, Sofia Hatch.

I see, I began.

. . .

You don't remember me, she interjected.

I'm sorry, I said.

It's okay, she said. Anyway, I was going to attend your parents' dinner tomorrow night, but I might not be able to come after all. Could you let them know?

All throughout high school, my mother would beg my

youngest brother and me to invite friends over for dinner, but we didn't have any. One day when I was sitting on my parents' living room couch in the post-suicide phase, I asked my mother what the most upsetting thing about my youngest brother's death was. She looked up from her crossword puzzle. She said he had moved out briefly to live closer to Marquette University, where he was supposedly attending law school. But his moving out was not what upset her, she claimed. What was most upsetting was that he had lied to her about having a roommate named Doug. She couldn't believe he had lied to her like that, he had made up a fictional person and given him a name!! It was a clue that he was far more ill than he had let on, she said, it was a sign he was approaching total derangement. Upon reflection, I realized that his lie was meant to assuage a particular anxiety she had about him not having any friends and being alone, *but those were her fears*, I said to myself, *those fears were never ours.*

Doug and I live downtown, my youngest brother had said.

She asked him to invite Doug over for dinner.

He said he'd think about it, but he never did.

So does Doug cook? my mother asked him.

Yeah, he told her. Doug cooks.

. . .

Are you still there? said Sofia Hatch.

I'm here, I said.

He looked me in the eye, my mother had said to me as I sat on the couch, and he said, *Yeah, Doug cooks.*

I might not be able to come tomorrow night, Sofia Hatch said again.

Thank you for sharing that with me, I said, repeating something I'd heard a man say on a reality-TV dating show.

Why are you laughing? Sofia Hatch said.

I'm not sure what you mean, I said.

You were laughing at something, but I don't know what. Are you okay?

I'm doing well, I said.

That's good.

. . .

Okay, she said. Goodbye.

I was grateful when she hung up.

Out of curiosity, I searched the name Sofia Hatch on my computer. There were no images of her. One of the few results was a digital guestbook for my youngest brother's funeral, now five years old, in which people had left their condolences.

I was his third-grade teacher, Patty Huffer wrote in 2013. *What a quiet young man taken too soon from us.*

He was a good neighbor, wrote Noni Malone. *He stood on a ladder and helped me change a lightbulb in my attic.*

I wished I had gotten to know him better. He didn't say much, wrote Ben Bennett.

He and his generosity will be missed, wrote Sofia Hatch. *Sending love to all the Morans.*

So she knew him, I thought, but in what capacity? Certainly well enough to attend his funeral and leave an entry in a digital guestbook. I wish I had gotten to know him better, I said to no one. What did I know about him? What did I really know? Instead of distinct scenes, I had impressions, fleeting ones, a flash of the green-and-gold-plaid couch I sat upon in his bedroom, where I watched him attempt to extract a brown thorn from his heel, the pondlike dampness of his car's fabric interior, the sight of his black Honda Accord pulling out of the driveway to go somewhere, but where? The stockiness of his body in his light blue polo shirt, his body's humidity, its own micro-climate, sweat stains under his arms, his thin hair limp against his skull. I never want to burden anyone, he once said, what kind of life would that be? I remembered he was sitting on his bed and unlacing his shoes, the same style of shoes he wore in grade school, black Sauconys with white laces, cheap and sturdy. Because of their thick cushioned soles, he appeared at least one or two inches taller than he was. He was a short Asian man. His hands were soft with stubby fingers. I tried to picture the three names he had written on them. The black caterpillars became jumbled, vaporous, floating in the air, a dragon's mouth exhaling puffs of cold smoke in a nearly forgotten dream.

The name Sofia Hatch shimmered brightly on my computer screen. Perhaps Sofia Hatch herself is a clue, I thought. I took out the envelope with the threatening smiley face letter. On it I wrote SOFIA HATCH and then her initials, SH.

SH as in shhhhh.

Silence, I said to no one.

The silence surrounding his suicide.

I wondered if someone was playing a joke on me or some kind of trick.

Perhaps someone had set a trap for me.

Perhaps Sofia Hatch was not a person but a trap.

I knew I needed to take matters into my own hands. I

rifled through the contents of the file box on my desk until I found my youngest brother's high school yearbook. I never understood the purpose of the yearbook even though I once served on the yearbook committee with the express purpose of ensuring that candid photos of myself never appeared in its pages. We think we are so important that we have to document the most horrifying period of our lives, and not only must we document it, we must publish it on glossy paper. The yearbook is worse than the graduation tassels because at least the tassels can be thrown away with impunity whereas everyone feels compelled to preserve the yearbook. I flipped through its pages, distracted by the pictures, every single person white except my youngest brother. Where were they now? The people from the yearbook went to church and ethnically themed summer fairs and stayed in the suburbs where they propagated themselves and they took their children to church, they kept adding more life to the planet. Whereas I left Milwaukee as soon as I could and had no children, my youngest brother stayed behind, and not only did he have no children, he took his own life. If I was an absolute zero, my brother was a negative one!!

As I flipped through the yearbook, I scanned its pages for the name Sofia Hatch. Was she the hypothetical girlfriend? She hadn't sounded very troubled on the phone. I could not locate one girl named Sofia, only a Sophie Rose Manley. With bureaucratic focus, I typed up a list of his female classmates on my computer and one by one looked up their social media information and phone numbers, email addresses, etc. Had I unwittingly typed one of the names of the three women?

Around midnight, someone knocked at my door, I heard the person call out my name, my actual name, Dan, are you in there? but I ignored them, I continued typing. By the time I was done, it was one in the morning.

I took out of my pocket the brochure from the Normandy Village Apartments, the invitation from the Ferrari Wing, and the letter with the threatening smiley face. I opened my carry-on suitcase and found the photo of my youngest brother dressed up as a detective. I put the brochure on top of the detective photo, the invitation, and letter, then I shuffled them like cards. I spread them out on the desk, searching for clues.

I inspected the trifold brochure of the Normandy Village Apartments, which featured photos that must've been taken at least five or ten years ago. Beige walls, beige carpet, beige furniture. The sterile, impersonal nature of the stock photos reminded me of my dorm in Iowa with its beds, bookshelves, and desks bolted to the floor. Silverfish and springtails had surged out of the cracks in the windowsills and danced above the pillow where I rested my head and dreamed of my escape. But where would I escape to? I had always thought a Swiss meadow sounded good. I was about to fold up the brochure, put it away in a drawer, and return to work on my psychological thriller in progress when a small photo caught my eye.

22

On the back of the third fold of the Normandy Village Apartments brochure was a picture of a young Asian man in a kitchen, holding in his arms a bag of groceries. Some carrot tops and a bunch of celery stuck up out of the brown paper bag. I was transfixed by the image of the young Asian man, wearing a light blue polo shirt and dark blue pants, almost like a Catholic grade school uniform. He appears to be in his late twenties. It was difficult to make out any distinct features of the young Asian man's face because the photo was so small, the size of a thumbprint, but his thin hair is flat on top of his head, as if molded by the shape of his baseball cap. He stands in an upright, cheerful, eager posture. On the opposite side of the kitchen, a woman with white hair holds out her arms either to receive the bag or embrace the young Asian man in gratitude for carrying her groceries. There was something familiar about the scene.

Then I remembered almost involuntarily how, when I moved from Wisconsin to Iowa, my youngest brother accompanied me and carried numerous black garbage bags of my belongings up three flights of stairs into my dorm room. My new roommate Mandy sat on her bed watching us, chewing gum, as mounds of black garbage bags began to accumulate on my side of the dorm room. She didn't offer to help as my youngest brother and I made numerous backbreaking trips up and down the stairs. Up and down we went until at last he and

I stood together in the doorframe of my room; he surveyed my new surroundings and told me my dorm looked like a place a person goes to die. And I laughed with him because I believed I might die there, I didn't have plans to, but, I remembered thinking, I wouldn't be surprised if it happened, either. What exactly was keeping me from dying in a double-occupancy dorm room in Iowa with Mandy from Dubuque?

But I didn't.

Die, that is.

My constant curiosity got in the way of my suicide.

And my youngest brother was the one who helped me move, from dorm to apartment to apartment, all over the Midwest. Iowa, Wisconsin, Minnesota. Any time a fresh crisis arose in my life, he was at my doorstep, ready to help, not necessarily because he wanted to but because I had summoned him.

The caption beneath the picture from the Normandy Village Apartments trifold brochure announced, *212 Alexander Lane, at your service!! Our management and tenants go above and beyond.* My youngest brother always went above and beyond, doing things for others and asking for nothing in return, I reflected, but what had I done for him? I tried to think of something. Of one simple thing.

Certainly there must have been . . .

Did you forget something? asked the threatening smiley face letter.

If I thought for a long time, I could detect a few traces of my own helpfulness scattered here and there. Breadcrumb traces. Flecks of helpfulness. At a granular level. Nothing substantial. Nothing concrete. I scrutinized the photo with intensity all night, scanning it, looking for clues, tormenting myself with vague speculations and questions about the nature of the photo, was it him, what was he doing in it, and why, so that by morning I became convinced the picture of the young Asian man holding the bag of groceries was a picture of my youngest brother.

My Korean adoptee brother.

My Kevin.

23

On September 28 I woke up.

Perhaps part of the problem with the first hundred pages I had completed from the perspective of a bumblebee taking a monstrous shit was a lack of forward momentum. The lack of forward momentum stemmed from an absence of cause and effect. Because the premise of the bumblebee pooping on the carpet was so odd, anything could happen, anything did, and therefore there was nothing for me, the writer, to anchor myself to emotionally or physically. Or the reader. Thomas Bernhard told me never to think of a reader when I was writing, unless the reader was Franz Kafka, then it was okay to think of the reader. These issues were on my mind as I woke up and went to my desk.

From my bedroom I could hear the coffeemaker beeping downstairs in the kitchen. Someone knocked on my bedroom door and called out, _______? Are you in there? Hello?

I did not respond. What was I supposed to say to that?

Whoever it was announced they were leaving in fifteen minutes.

Are you planning on getting dressed today? said the voice. Are you coming with us, or are you going to mope around in a bathrobe all day?

I have always been liable to spend an entire day home in a grayish bathrobe.

How did the person know?

The Normandy Village Apartments brochure sat on my desk taunting me.

In the clarity of the morning light that streamed through my childhood bedroom windows, new details emerged. In the picture, my youngest brother's dark brown pebble eyes were slits, his mouth a thin line lightly upturned at the corners, an ambiguous smile, the barest suggestion of an outline of a nose. The photograph was of such grainy resolution, but upon careful inspection, I detected an aura of resignation, anger, and inertia masked behind my brother's cheerful, helpful, upright posture.

It had been five years since his suicide, and I could hardly recall the details of his face. And it occurred to me, after reading all of Thomas Bernhard's work, I could not recall one description of a human face, I could not point to a single description of a facial feature or characteristic, the color of a person's eyes in a certain light, the shape their mouth made when they were trying to suppress sadness or anger, the subtle movement of an eyebrow raised, the other lowered, the clench of a jaw, a wriggling worm of a forehead vein, I couldn't remember any of that in Thomas Bernhard's pages, his thousands of Bernhardian pages. Everyone knows the more space something takes up on the page, the more significance it has. Going off this logic, it follows that the human face meant nothing to Thomas Bernhard. People don't need a description of a face, it doesn't matter, they'll just picture the author's, which is what I taught my own troubled youth.

Now, in hindsight, I wondered if I should've looked at my own brother's face more carefully when he was alive.

Perhaps it would have told me something.

But what?

What would his face have told me?

24

A few days after my youngest brother died, I heard my parents talking quietly in the kitchen about the possibility of hiring a private investigator named David Dunn. My father wanted David Dunn to look into unexplained matters regarding my youngest brother's activities leading up to his suicide. That day, many years ago, I got up from my observation post on the couch and peeked into the kitchen. My parents were at the kitchen table with a stack of papers and a manila folder, probably my youngest brother's bank statements. Your mother and I are thinking of working with a man named David Dunn, my father said. Things aren't adding up. He was talking with my middle brother Matthias on speakerphone. The two men were making investigative plans without me, even though Matthias was thousands of miles away. Matthias said hiring a detective sounded like a good idea, given the strange circumstances.

My father asked Matthias if he had noticed anything different about my youngest brother's behavior in the last year, if he had observed any extravagant spending habits or if my youngest brother had mentioned the names of any *new or questionable friends*. At the time, I did not yet know about his *constellation of women*. I don't know, Matthias said. Have you talked with _______ about any of this? Maybe she knows something? It was quiet in the kitchen. Your mother and I don't think it's a good idea to involve your sister, my father said. There are certain matters we should keep between us.

Like what? I wondered. She's not doing well, he continued. She just sits on the living room couch, and when she isn't sitting in silence, she puts her hand in front of her mouth to conceal her laughter. I don't know what she's laughing at. Truthfully, I always thought she would be the one to die first, my middle brother said. I could hear my mother clear her throat, blow her nose into a tissue. Then my father started to say things about David Dunn, how no one could hide their past from a man like David Dunn. He has a talent for reading faces, he can tell when a face is full of lies.

As I stared at the picture in the Normandy Village Apartments brochure, I realized I was asking myself the wrong questions. What my brother's face would've told me was of no consequence now. No, I needed to ask: what did his face, his Korean adoptee face, have to do with the Normandy Village Apartments?

I would need to go back to the leasing office and interrogate the woman behind the counter about who had produced the brochure and why my youngest brother was involved.

On my phone I was scrolling through the Normandy Village Google reviews when I came across one by a tenant with the initials KM:

> *one star out of four*
>
> *The carpet is beige. The walls are beige. It's clean and there is a lot of storage. At first this apartment seemed like an ok place to live. It's quiet and residential with easy access to restaurants and a grocery store and GameStop, but new management took over and now*

it's a dump. It's a place people go to die, hahahaha. I'm looking for a way to get out. I don't want to be here.
—KM

It was from September 20, 2013.

Five years ago.

A week before his death.

The initials KM, could it be?

The plain language and flatness of the voice was everything I remembered about my brother. I looked him up in the White Pages. It had never occurred to me to do that before. It listed his name and two addresses, my childhood home, and 212 Alexander Lane, but it did not specify a particular unit number.

So, instead of attending Marquette University Law School and living briefly with a roommate Doug who cooked, my youngest brother had secretly lived in the Normandy Village, not far from our childhood home, and not only had he rented a unit, he had also posed in its promotional materials. That alone, the posing, the stock photo posing, went against everything I thought I knew about him and his debilitating shyness and preference for total solitude.

He had lived there.

And now he was speaking to me from the dead.

I went into the empty kitchen to help myself to a cup of coffee. My parents' phone rang, and instead of letting it ring multiple times, I answered it on the second ring.

25

Hello? I said.

Good morning, said a woman. Do I have the pleasure of speaking with Paul Moran?

Is this Millie Baker from Pope Pius High School? I said.

Yes, who is this?

Millie, it's Dan Moran, the author. We spoke yesterday about my reading. I want to give a reading in honor of my youngest brother's memory.

Right. Is Paul Moran there? I'd like to speak to him.

But why? Why are you calling my parents at their house?

Her voice was muffled. She was talking to someone with her hand over the phone.

Sorry, sir, she said. After we talked, I realized I did not have any updated information for Paul and Mary Moran besides a phone number. I want to see if they'd be interested in receiving our free alumni magazine.

I know they're not interested in subscribing to another magazine, I said. They already get *Wisconsin Monthly*, *National Geographic*, *Better Homes & Gardens*. They're very frugal people, you know. They're cheap.

The alumni magazine is free, she said. I just need an updated address for them and we can get the ball rolling.

They're about to move. They won't live here anymore. Did you listen to my voicemail?

I'm sure someone will get back to you if and when it's

appropriate, Millie said. I should go now. Thank you for your time.

I need to talk with Matilda Pierre about the logistics of her reading. What's her number? It's imperative I speak with her.

I'm sorry, Mr. Moran, but I can't give out people's contact information without their permission, she said.

Is the reading with Matilda Pierre free and open to the public? I said.

I can't stop you from attending a reading if that's what you feel you need to do, she said.

I'm also a detective, I said.

SIR, I need to go now!! Millie said. Have a good day.

Our conversation ended. I hung up the landline. I thought I heard footsteps echoing down the hall then a door slam shut. A grinding of dull machinery. It was the garage door closing. A car was disappearing down the driveway, it had a Colorado license plate, but I couldn't see the driver. Had someone been in the kitchen listening in on my conversation with Millie Baker? Was it my brother Matthias?

26

There are two sides to everyone, I said to myself. For years, I had seen only one side of my youngest brother. I did not know about the other side, the man who chose to live at 212 Alexander Lane in the Normandy Village Apartments, I could only imagine him. I did not know of the man who chose to pose in a brochure, the man who may have had a troubled girlfriend, the man who may have had a whole constellation of women, the man who wrote down the names of three women on his hand sometime leading up to the night he died, the three black caterpillar names traveling up and down his fingers on the verge of a total transformation.

To make sense of things, I would need to speak with the people from his past, the people who had seen the other side of him, the one I knew nothing about. I sat at my childhood desk and opened a blank email on my computer. I came up with the subject line: MY SPECIAL READING IS TONIGHT. I sipped my coffee as I composed my email invitation to his friends and acquaintances from his high school. To compose an email can be as treacherous as writing a book, I thought, there are so many traps one may fall into such as overexplaining, unnecessary apologies and complaints, backtracking, digressions, humorless anecdotes, etc. I combed through my email looking for traps, errors, and typos before I pressed send to the classmates from my youngest brother's yearbook.

Dear friend,

I am a local author and, even more importantly, the oldest sibling of Kevin Moran, former classmate of yours. I would like to invite you to a reading in his honor at his alma mater, Pope Pius High School, on Sept 28 at 6 p.m. along with another local reader, Matilda Pierre, a feminist nature writer. I know it's short notice, but it's a wonderful opportunity to catch up and share memories of my brother. I wrote my book in his honor and am excited to share it with you. Please support a local author and help me remember him.

Dan Moran

At the bottom of my email, I included links to several favorable articles about my book and my Goodreads page. I would have included an endorsement from Thomas Bernhard, but I didn't have one. A few months ago, he gave a reading in Manhattan upon the release of his latest novel, and during the Q&A after the reading, I took meticulous notes, hoping he might say something about how I had studied with him, *his star pupil*, author of a book, a published one. Of course, my name never came up; whenever one strains to listen for one's name, one's name hardly comes up, if ever. Besides, he had a stated policy of treating all his students the same. At his reading in Manhattan, I stood in a dark corner of the bookstore where no one talked to me. I didn't approach him or ask him to sign my book; he had not responded to my emails in years.

Some people claimed Thomas Bernhard was the coldest man they'd ever met, completely cut off from other humans and emotionally aloof, but that wasn't my experience of him. Thomas Bernhard taught me what it meant to think and act freely. Instead of stepping off a stool, a chair, a bridge, I would sit next to Thomas Bernhard during his office hours as he looked over my pages and immediately threw them into the trash. Or he would point to a sentence and say, *This is a good one, write more of these.* And during those office hours, I learned what was a good sentence and what was not, I learned one doesn't need to describe a face or a chair, one doesn't need to move a character across a room, one doesn't need to force a character to sit at a table, characters don't need to go to the bathroom, they don't get tired the way real humans do, they don't need to eat anything unless you want to write about food, etc. I learned if one is unsure about how to end a chapter, one can make the narrator fall asleep, then start a new one. And I'll never know exactly what he saw in me, perhaps he recognized a sympathetic ear for his characteristically relentless digressions and ruminations. Perhaps I had reminded him of someone from his past, who can say. And I remembered, with some shame and embarrassment, how I had asked him to continue to meet with me after I had graduated. Could we still meet in your office twice a month? I had asked, and only now, as a teacher myself, do I understand how appalling my request was, for him to continue to meet with me for free. He never responded. And some people might find it hard to believe I managed to write a book, a published one, knowing what they know about me, but during my time in graduate school, I learned it's the most demented and mentally unwell writers who have the easiest time getting their books published, even the most awful, unhinged, stupid, and neurotic person can write and publish a book, then step into a roomful of strangers and talk about it and persuade them to buy it. Almost all my writer friends are suicidal in some way, I reflected, mostly in a soft, ambient way, their suicidal thoughts humming in the background like a refrigerator or a noise machine, while others are *openly suicidal, more suicidal-forward.* And whenever I admitted to Thomas Bernhard that I was afraid I would discover I didn't have the necessary talent to write about suicide or transracial adoption, Thomas Bernhard told me it didn't matter. He told me talent was beside the point. Unless someone was a genius, then it was the main thing. Over the course of the hundreds of office hours I spent with him, he said that when writing a book, we must be able to see the book from an unimaginable distance like a tall building erected in the middle of a grassy field. If the foundation is poor, the building collapses. There are infinite ways for a book to be wrong, he said. And there's only about one or two ways for a book to be right; it's probably a matter of luck in terms of landing on the one or two possible ways for the book to be right, but not many people like to think about that. It's easier to think about revision and plot and worldbuilding and character development and reversals and rate of revelation. It's not productive to think about writing as luck or incantation or a spell when one can think about writing as architecture, writing as construction, writing as stonemasonry, writing as a system of helical piers. I avoided the ones who conceive of writing as construction and extensive planning, *the three-ring-binder bureaucrats who write their three-ring-binder novels.* I preferred to align with the ones who believe writing is like standing on one side of an ancient forest and on the other side is everyone you've ever known, the living, the dead, waiting to say things to you. How to cross to the other side? One way is through relentless observation, along with writing the book in one's head before writing it down. Most days, instead of meeting on campus, he instructed the class to walk to the subway station and sit on a bench and record what we saw. There was also a hotel lobby downtown he told us to go to. A concert hall open to the public in the afternoon. A farmhouse an hour-long bus ride away. A swimming pool at the top floor of a history museum. A boxing gym where every guy was at best a fifty-to-one underdog. Thomas Bernhard never went with us to any of these places; I have no idea what he did while we loitered in the subway with our notebooks or sat in leather chairs in the hotel lobby. Perhaps he went home.

Later, when I became an adjunct instructor at the private arts college in Brooklyn, I tried Thomas Bernhard's observation technique with my troubled youth, I instructed them to go to the Fulton Mall, but I ended that practice when one of my troubled youth never came back. She never came back from the Fulton Mall. To this day, I don't know what happened, even though I made polite and subtle inquiries.

It's possible, I now reflected, she did not enjoy my class and dropped it.

27

I have never been a man prone to digression, I have always believed in the path ahead, the path to press on and move forward. I was at my childhood desk, looking out my bedroom window, when I spotted a silver SUV making its way down the driveway. Before I knew what was happening, I heard the doorbell ring, disrupting my momentum. Because I had on my gray bathrobe, I remained in my room. I waited at the window until I saw a woman walking back toward her silver SUV with a straight, stiff, birdlike posture, and with horror, I realized it was The Chocolate Goose woman.

What was she doing at my parents' house without their knowledge?

Instead of getting into her SUV, she pivoted and strode toward the side entrance of my childhood home as if she were familiar with its layout and how to get inside. I fled to my youngest brother's room, where from his window I could look down at the decorative Oriental gate and the path along the side entrance to observe her.

I stepped across the threshold and for a moment I didn't know where I was.

My youngest brother's room had been transformed into a guest room and there was a formal, solemn, museumlike quality to its arrangement. Although the room had once been crammed floor to ceiling with his belongings, DVDs, books, CDs, video games, nothing left in the room was connected to him. All evidence of his life in the room, almost thirty years, had been removed. What remained: a blue armchair with a matching ottoman and a floor lamp, a double mattress in a wrought-iron bed frame, a small mahogany nightstand with a landline, a framed oil painting of a lake enclosed by a forest on an autumn day, the rays of the sun cutting through some clouds wrapped around purple mountains in the background. It was a painting typical of what may be found in a roadside motel, the ones my parents would force us to stay in on our summer road trips.

Above the nightstand I noticed a newspaper article pinned to the wall, a plain yellowing piece of newspaper cut out carefully. Sometime during the last five years, my mother had decided to display this article. She was the sole decorator of my childhood home. I noticed she had written his name in the corner in blue pen, her old-fashioned cursive looping delicately in the lower-right-hand corner: *Kevin Moran, 1993.*

I LIKE LIVING HERE was the headline.

My youngest brother had written a letter to the editor of the local newspaper.

There wasn't enough time to read it, not with The Chocolate Goose woman roving around outside. I unpinned the article, folded it, and put it in my pocket. Through my brother's bedroom window, I scanned the yard for The Chocolate Goose woman. Through the treetops, I could see her attempting to unlatch the Oriental gate. I opened the window.

What are you doing at my parents' house? I shouted. What exactly do you think you're doing here?

The silver SUV remained stationary in my childhood driveway, obstructing my ability to leave the house. I got dressed and went downstairs, and as I passed the mudroom, I could see The Chocolate Goose woman standing outside, peering in through the window. Her hooded falcon eyes spotted me.

Matthias!! she called out, smiling. It's so nice to see you again.

. . .

Did you hear that crazy man shouting a few minutes ago? So strange!! She laughed.

I told her I was on my way out and I needed her to move the SUV.

I'm just dropping off some things, she said. I'll be quick, I promise. By the way, will I see your wonderful sister tonight?

She was beaming.

My sister? I said. Tonight? What's tonight?

Yes, tonight, she said. For the memorial dinner. Like we talked about yesterday.

They're having the dinner at my childhood home? I said.

She laughed as if I had made a joke.

Will you be a dear and open the garage door for me? she said.

I wondered if the memorial dinner would conflict with my reading at Pope Pius High School. My roommate Julie once said to me, Don't worry, ______. You worry so much, and all your worries take over your thoughts. Worrying and thinking all the time, she said, doesn't it hurt your head?

I opened the garage door. I watched The Chocolate Goose

woman unload several metal trays from the SUV into a storage refrigerator. I didn't offer to help, I didn't want to listen to her explain the proper way to load them. When she finished, she waved and got into her SUV. As I sat in the driver's seat of my brother's car, I glanced at my phone and saw my brother's one-star review of the Normandy Village Apartments. When I opened the map, it was already directing me back to the complex.

What had he been doing there?

I was backing out of the long and curving driveway when a police car pulled up to my childhood home, the lights flashing but silent. I stopped. A blond police officer with broad shoulders got out. She waited for me to roll down the window and leaned in.

What's going on here, sir? We got a call about a possible noise disturbance. One of your neighbors said they heard a man screaming out a window. What's your name?

My name is Dan Moran, I said, and I think there's been a misunderstanding. Everything is fine. My parents are Paul and Mary Moran.

The police officer scrutinized my face.

I've never seen you here, she said. Do you live with them?

I'm visiting, I said. I visit them about once every five years.

When I turned to make direct eye contact with her, she took a few steps back as if she needed to get an objective look.

Can you please step out of the car? she said.

What's the trouble, exactly, Officer? Did I do something wrong?

Sir, I need you to step out of the car right now.

I opened the door and got out. I put my hands up even though she didn't ask me to.

Wow, she said quietly.

What? I said.

You look like him, she whispered.

Who?

The police officer sucked in her breath.

Your brother, she said.

Matthias? I said.

I let my hands drop to my sides.

Your brother, she repeated. Kevin. He took my class in the citizen's police academy years ago with your parents.

Oh, I said. My youngest brother. You knew him.

I remember him because I was there . . . when it happened. I knocked on your parents' door that night. I was there.

. . .

There are no violent crimes in this suburb, she said. So when something like that happens, it leaves an impression.

. . .

It was a terrible night, of course, she added. It's the worst kind of night. We kept calling them on the phone, but no one picked up. So we drove here, and we had to go up to that front door and knock in the middle of the night. You see, it's the middle of the night and they're upstairs sleeping, your parents are up there dreaming and it's dark out. No one expects to hear a knock like that in the middle of the night. And I remember it took them a long time, an eternity, really, to come down to the door. While I was waiting for them to make their way downstairs, I kept pounding my fist against the door, because what else could I do? What I'll remember more than anything was knocking at their door. To have to knock like that, to wait for them to come down, to have to tell them, to have to explain . . . It haunts you.

My mind was spinning. It was as if my brother had just died and she was telling me about his death for the first time.

It was possible she had looked at his body. My brother's body in the black Honda Accord. She saw him. There were so many questions I wanted to ask her, where to begin, where to begin, perhaps with the three names, because she would have seen them on his hand, the three senseless names, because at this point in my investigation they had become senseless to me. I asked her if she saw them, if she remembered what was written on his hand in black marker.

The letters were like fuzzy black caterpillars, I explained.

I don't remember that, she said.

Are you sure?

I explained I had reopened my investigation due to crucial information that had been withheld from me five years ago.

Withheld from me by my parents, I clarified. Not by the local police.

It's an unofficial investigation, I added.

The police officer did a slight double take, then her face returned to a neutral, blank expression. The male partner waiting in the car called out, Jeanette, it's time to go.

I see, she said. Well, good luck with that, Mr. Moran.

28

From my childhood home to the Normandy Village Apartments was a direct route that cut through an old arboretum.

It took me ten minutes to get to the apartment complex. The garbage must have been picked up early that morning because the brown dumpsters were empty; the boxes scattered near them had been cleared away. My youngest brother could have gone anywhere in the world, but he'd chosen to live ten minutes away from our childhood home.

I parked his car in front of the Normandy Village Apartments leasing office. I felt my phone vibrate. A text from my mother: *Had a very nice lunch at Grimaldi's*, she wrote. She sent me a photo of my middle brother Matthias, his daughter, and his wife, the one everyone adored. I never knew what to say when she sent me photos of my middle brother Matthias. I knew she wanted me to talk about him with affection and warmth; she wanted proof she had raised her Korean adoptees correctly.

Just checking in to make sure you decided to get dressed today, she texted. *We're going to mass later. I suppose you don't want to come . . .*

At the leasing office for the Normandy Village Apartments, instead of the middle-aged woman on her phone, there was a young man in a red polo shirt behind the counter. I asked if he had any information about a former tenant, Kevin Moran.

Who? he said. Is that a celebrity or something?

A door behind the counter area opened. A bathroom or inner office, perhaps. The middle-aged woman stepped out. Yesterday she had on a lilac blouse; today it was teal, patterned with bright yellow butterflies.

Did I hear you say the name Kevin Moran? she said.

That's right.

I knew him, she said. Who are you?

What do you know about him? I said. What can you tell me?

You were here yesterday afternoon. You were upset about a letter. You tell people you're a detective.

I'd like to know which unit Kevin Moran used to live in.

Why?

It's important to me, I said.

But why? Why do you care? What difference does it make?

I didn't know how to answer her questions in a reasonable manner, so I pivoted. I took out the trifold brochure and smoothed it across the counter. The brochure had become wrinkled and creased from my many examinations of it.

Do you know what company produced this brochure? I asked.

As the woman and the young man studied it, I became agitated to think about a stranger looking at the picture of my brother in the trifold brochure and to imagine what kinds of false conclusions they might draw about him and his life. In the image, his eyes were thin, dark, lifeless lines; unlike the detective photo from our childhood, it had no eye of inquiry.

Seeing the brochure spread out on the counter, almost as

if it were undergoing a forensic examination, I realized he had been suicidal in this photo. I was sure of it.

In this picture he had already begun to formulate his suicide plan.

To park his black Honda Accord in front of the hospital.

To wipe his laptop of everything except his suicide letter, which he composed seconds before he made his decision.

READ_ME!!.docx

Double exclamation.

To sit in the driver's seat and shoot himself in the head.

And I was the only one who could detect the rage and hopelessness underneath his cheerful posture and uncertain smile.

Probably someone who works in this office, said the woman. Why does it matter?

The young man in this picture is not with us anymore, I said. He's dead. They say he died unexpectedly, but what they really mean whenever they say that is he took his own life.

After I said the word *dead*, a new energy came into the office. By uttering the phrase *took his own life*, I had upset the woman behind the counter.

I knew Kevin Moran, she said. He was a really good kid. A really good one. Always paid his rent on time. Very quiet. Clean. I remember hearing what happened to him. It was violent and horrible. Why are you coming in here and bringing this up? What's wrong with you?

I was troubled by her questioning, particularly her question of why, why was I doing this, why was I digging up such *a violent and horrible* event from the past. She wanted to know why I was taking an event that was, from her perspective, completely over and settled, and now reanimating it with my questions; she had turned the tables on me, demanding concrete answers. Why, why, why? Who did I think I was, to go over this story from years before, to rehash it, to tell it again, *that same old suicide story*, to bring it back to life? I thought of the authors who did that, the ones who wrote the same story over and over instead of using their imagination and radically reinventing themselves with each book, they chose to tell the same story, orbiting, stalking, obsessing, drawing closer and closer to their wound and their desire for it, picking at their scabs; writers who did this were probably the least defensible.

I'm not doing this because I want to, I said, but because I don't have a choice.

There's something wrong with you, she said.

This brochure is a lie, I said, and pointed at his picture. You need to fix this immediately. Print a retraction or a correction or get rid of it. Stop giving these out to people for free. Everything about it is wrong. He never ate carrots or celery. He only pretended to like helping people. All of this is a lie, a grotesque misrepresentation, a facade. And his facade fell away so fast. You have no idea how unhappy he really was.

I think I understand, she said. I think we all got the message.

Without another word, she left the office. She had turned away just as my youngest brother had turned away from me before he died, I thought, the way he had physically pushed me away the last time I saw him when I tried to give him a hug; he had kept me in the dark regarding his suicide plans, lied to me about who he was and what he was doing, lied about everything in his life, his occupations, hopes, and dreams, and now, five years later, I felt at times as if I remembered hardly anything about him, he was a figure from my past slowly dissolving over the years into nothingness. That's what they mean when they say someone is dead, I thought, the person dissolves into nothingness and you can't bring them back.

29

Part of me was troubled by the leasing office woman's pointed critiques, her questioning of me and what I was doing, particularly her question of *why*. I rushed out of the leasing office and drove to the far end of the Normandy Village Apartments where Zachary lived, where I had crouched beneath the windowsill the night before and investigated. I felt a sense of urgency and unease, that 212 Alexander Lane was the key to what was happening to me. The phone calls, the photos, the letter. The constellation of women. The three names on my brother's hand. Perhaps someone who lived here knew him. I needed to get inside the building, I thought, to investigate further. I would wait until a person came along and opened the entrance door. I checked my inbox to see if anyone had responded to my reading invitation at Pope Pius High School. There was exactly one email reply from a Joshua Hoolahan.

Hey, who is this? I don't know a Dan Moran. I remember Matthias, Kevin, and a sister. Who are you? Thanks.

Joshua Hoolahan
V.P., All-American Plumbing

"I'm the pipe whisperer"—Josh

I didn't respond to Joshua Hoolahan, *the pipe whisperer.* I once wrote that sometimes a nonresponse is itself a response. And I still believe that, I reflected. At last, a UPS man approached and buzzed an intercom. I stepped out of the car and pretended to stretch my legs. The entrance opened wide, and as the door began to close, almost in slow motion, I slipped indoors and walked in the opposite direction of the UPS man toward what I believed was Zachary's apartment, down a red-carpeted hall smelling of patchouli and sage, a scent that transported me instantly to the carpeted staircase, cramped and winding, that led up to my Korean adoptee therapist's office.

Why are you doing this? Tina asked me in a pantomime of the middle-aged woman in the butterfly blouse. Who is this helping?

As I proceeded down the hallway, I put my ear up to each door but heard nothing, not a single human voice or sound. A unit had its door propped open with a plastic bin of cleaning supplies and rags. Although there was furniture, it was of the impersonal variety, overstock from a hotel or a discount furniture store. Books without words. Overstuffed beige plaid couches, lightweight and easy to push from one side of the room to the other. A bowl of fake pears. The windows of the apartment looked out at the placid expanse of the parking lot. It was ugly and depressing, but to me it had transformed into something magical and strange because it was once where my youngest brother had parked his car without anyone's knowledge. It wasn't an ordinary parking lot. It was my youngest brother's secret parking lot.

My phone buzzed.

Hey old friend :) It's Nina. Great to see you yesterday. What are you doing tonight

There was that phrase again, *old friend*. Was that Nina's way of insinuating she had figured out my identity? Had she looked up the name Matthias Moran online and seen a photo of my middle brother on LinkedIn? I replied that I was busy. I didn't say anything about my reading at my brother's high school.

As I put my phone back into my pocket, my fingers brushed against a piece of paper. The newspaper clipping. My mother's cursive in the corner.

I LIKE LIVING HERE was the headline to my youngest brother's letter to the editor of the village newspaper. It was quaint to think of our suburb as a village, with its grand population of seven thousand people and fewer than five Asians. Now that *the three Korean adoptees* had moved out or died, it was possible there were none. In two concise paragraphs, my brother described how our village was an ideal place for a nine-year-old boy. Within walking distance, there was a grocery store, a park, The Chocolate Goose. At night, one fell asleep to the gentle sounds of the distant trains traveling south to Chicago. Of special interest for my youngest brother was the ancient water-powered granary mill that was once operated by twin brothers and now was open to the public for tours guided by a local historian named Mrs. Kowalski. *Everyone should take a tour of the mill if they want to know what everlasting peace feels like!* he wrote. But perhaps the best thing about our suburb was the lack of crime.

There are no violent crimes here, he wrote. *It's safe.*

I shuddered.

I thought of what the broad-shouldered police officer had said.

I could hear the police officer banging her fist on my parents' door.

The two of them took a long time to make their way down the staircase.

Did they already know what she was about to say? Were they prepared?

Had they known all along what he was headed for?

Or had it been a shock?

It must've been a shock, I speculated, because shortly after my brother died, my father's dark brown hair went white.

When my brother wrote the letter to the editor, he must've been in third or fourth grade.

The best years of his life.

He had spent the last year of his life in an apartment that might have resembled the model unit I was standing in. In the bedroom was a double bed with a beige plaid comforter that matched the couches. I sat down and closed my eyes. What did I hope to find here in this blankness?

When I opened them, my eyes rested on a painting on the wall facing the bed. Instead of the typical pastel-colored abstract print, someone had hung an amateurish oil portrait of a woman's face. I was surprised to see artwork made by an actual human. Behind the woman's wan smile was a grim psychic cosmology, and I couldn't help but remember the woman my middle brother Matthias brought home for Christmas.

As I looked at the painting, I had an involuntary memory of that Christmas Eve many years ago. Matthias had gathered my parents and several relatives in the basement and said he had something to show us. He hooked up his computer to the television. As it turned out, the woman with the white braid was an amateur artist.

Without an introduction, she began to click through a slideshow of her work.

The paintings were thrift store and estate sale finds—garish, amateurish portraits of white faces: a child in a dress with a ruffled collar, someone's lover with a sour expression, a next-door neighbor who was somehow simultaneously childish and time-ravaged, an avuncular type wearing a hunting cap, a teenage girl with spiky brown hair that looked plastic.

The woman with the white braid had painted on top of each white face a very small, thick grotesque Asian face, mask-like, staring out at the viewer with wide-awake, surprised eyes. A cruel, mocking self-portrait.

As she clicked through her paintings, she talked about being a Korean adoptee and how the face within a face was meant to represent a double consciousness, a portrait of being caught in between someone's already manufactured reality and her own experience of alienation as a displaced Korean.

Which face was more real? I remembered her asking my family and relatives. No one dared to say a word. It was clear none of them understood what she was asking, not even Matthias. Each face was a representation of the grotesque in its own way, she explained, but the source of the psychic power of the paintings was the contrast drawn between the two faces. The space between the contrast was open to interpretation. Her paintings gestured at the adoptee experience in a surreal and haunting manner. In these emotionally volatile landscapes, she continued to explain, there was a fragile quality, an almost defenseless posturing.

She said she did not expect mass popularity or commercial success. She did not desire any approval from the so-called art world. She refused to have a website. She did not rent studio space. She did not have business cards to give out.

She said she made her art only for herself and for other Korean adoptees.

No one else.

Which was why she was in our basement that Christmas Eve.

She wanted to show her portraits to the three Korean adoptees, my middle brother, my youngest brother, and me.

Very painterly, I commented, because no one else was saying anything. Very painterly indeed, I murmured from a dark corner where I stood with my arms crossed, as if we were in a studio critique.

These paintings are interesting to look at, added my mother.

The way she said *interesting* suggested she didn't know what other word to say.

Could you go back a couple images? said my youngest brother.

He was standing next to me, riveted by what he was seeing. I couldn't remember what the image was, what he wanted to look at again. It didn't seem important at the time. In hindsight, I wished I had paid more attention. Perhaps it wasn't the image, I reflected. Perhaps it didn't matter which portrait it was. Perhaps it was the question itself, his interest in her work.

30

I caught myself starting to speculate about the woman with the white braid when, in reality, I didn't know her name, who she was, I hardly remembered her. There I was, getting lost in my fabrications again.

Wake up, Dan, I said to myself.

I went into the kitchen with its plain brown wooden cabinets from the seventies. I opened drawers and discovered backup fake pears and handfuls of crumbs. There was a single bag of grocery-store-brand white rice in one of the cabinets. Plain long-grain white rice, the kind of rice my youngest brother liked, one of two foods he ate voluntarily. My mother used to make mounds of white rice and mounds of white chicken to feed us, the whitest Korean people on the planet. And for a moment I could convince myself that this was where my youngest brother had lived. The impersonal furniture. Fake fruit that never rots. White rice entombed in the cabinet. Crumbs in the drawer. Windows looking out onto nothing, only the parking lot, a transitional space, a fresh start, a clean slate.

31

At the mall of my childhood, I tried on a series of light blue polo shirts at a men's clothing store. I wanted something nice to wear to my reading at Pope Pius High School; I needed to appear trustworthy in order to draw out the ones who once knew my youngest brother and have them submit to my questioning. I had not bought a brand-new shirt in several years. I preferred not to spend money on clothes or my appearance. I looked at myself in the full-length mirror inside the dressing room. Over a year on testosterone and I had somehow transformed into a combination of my two brothers, even though none of us was biologically related. I was about five-eight, taller than my youngest brother, who was five-four but shorter than Matthias, who must have been at least five-ten but was slight and willowy for a man. My hair was thicker and coarser than theirs, and my skin was far worse, greasy and acne-prone, but my teeth were straighter than my youngest brother's and my shoulders were thicker and wider than Matthias's. Like my middle brother Matthias, I had worked in retail at the mall more than twenty years ago. Unlike him, I wore a green apron and sold puzzles, games, incense, animal figurines, calendars, blankets, Beanie Babies, etc., at the nature and incense store. One day a very tall woman with excellent posture came into the store. She asked me what I wanted to do with my life. I said I wanted to go to as many Fiona Apple concerts as possible, I wanted to follow Fiona Apple around on tour. I was sixteen or seventeen. The tall woman looked me straight in the eye and told me that my dreams would come true if I joined the Marines because the Marines got to travel the world. As I walked through the mall, I was certain I would run into someone I once knew. Or that someone would mistake me for Matthias, or else for my other brother, the dead one, the one who was gone. I expected someone to clap me on the back and say, Kevin Moran!! What have you done with yourself all these years? But no one did, no one approached me except a man at a kiosk who tried to sell me an intricate back massager and an ergonomic neck pillow. In my head I began to rehearse my speech, my rebuttal to whatever my middle brother Matthias might say about me. I thought of the differences between us, what kept us apart all these years. My posture was straighter than my youngest brother's but more stooped than Matthias's. Whereas my youngest brother was suicidal and succumbed to his suicidal ideation, I was only sometimes suicidal, and I exploited it by writing about it and publishing my writing. A writer friend who read my book once said he couldn't tell the difference between the two of us, my youngest brother and me, he thought we were *the same character*. The main difference, the most significant difference, is I'm still here and he isn't. I am writing and he is dead. For the last five years I've managed to keep myself alive. But how? My youngest brother liked Kobe Bryant's killer instinct, and I preferred Hakeem Olajuwon's intelligence; most people would disagree, but I believed if they had played one-on-one, Hakeem would've won easily due to his length and his panther-like agility. My earwax was lighter in color; both of my brothers had thick, wet, brown-orange earwax, and I knew this because I would go through the trash in our shared bathroom and look at their used Q-tips; my earwax was dry, flaky, and pale yellow, almost translucent, like the delicate wings of a golden flying insect from a fairy tale. My youngest brother had trouble falling asleep and staying asleep, and Matthias could fall asleep anywhere; I was somewhere between the two. If I was tired, I could fall asleep on the train just lightly enough to wake up at the exact moment the train pulled into my stop. Lucky. I was lucky enough that one day my biological father in Korea decided he was tired of feeling guilty and reached out to the orphanage to let them know to contact me immediately. He said he would answer any questions I had and that he hoped to see my face before he died. That's all he wanted, he wrote, just to see my face before he died. He was a very simple man, I remembered, and had a flair for the dramatic. My youngest brother was stocky; I was thin and had trouble putting on weight, but after testosterone I gained thirty pounds and now had to manage my weight. My middle brother was thin and unremarkable except for his eyebrows, which were arched and villain-like. When I was in seventh grade, my middle brother began to touch my leg when we sat next to each other on the basement couch watching television at night, after I had finished my kitchen cleanup duties. Back then I wore a long T-shirt with Umbros to bed. He would run his finger up and down the length of my leg even after I asked him to stop. His finger had the lightness of a house spider; I never knew when it would appear. Up and down the spider went as my leg hairs stood on end. I hadn't started to shave my legs yet because my mother would not allow it. Later I would resort to sitting cross-legged on the floor with a pillow on my lap, a manner of sitting that I have continued with to this day. I had heard my mother claim that people asked her what race my middle brother was, they could not tell, whereas my youngest brother was blatantly East Asian. I met an Indigenous Russian at a party once and she immediately took me aside and asked me if I was an Indigenous Russian. She was excited. She showed me photos on her phone of what Indigenous Russians look like; and by the end of the party, she had convinced me I was an Indigenous Russian. My youngest brother spent the last third of his life searching for his biological mother. He told me she had a round face, that was all he'd discovered about her. It was in his adoption file. His biological mother was short and had a round face. That's it. Just like my round face, he had said. And he seemed happy for a moment, that he resembled her. Then his smile disappeared, as if he needed to suppress his happiness, as if there were something dangerous about it. He didn't want to have hope, not even for a moment. I had emailed him a photo of my biological sister a week before he took his own life. Was it a coincidence? Or was the photo of my biological sister what sent him over the edge into the abyss? Upon examination of my sister's photo, I came to understand I possessed something he didn't: a family narrative, a beginning, middle, and end. For the first third of his life, he feared his mother would show up during the middle of a school day and demand he return with her to Korea. For the last third of his life, he feared she would never show up at all. My middle brother Matthias searched for his biological mother and made an appearance on a television show in Korea, *I Miss That Person.* No one came forward. Unlike the two of them, I never commenced any kind of search. Mine sought me out. My brothers searched and searched and found nothing, whereas I searched for nothing and was found. There was something optimistic about my brothers' searching. But at what cost did their searches come if they ended up with nothing? I had risked nothing and ended up with answers to my existential questions. For more than three decades I had no idea who I was. Then one day a person, my biological father to be exact, reached out and said to me, I know exactly who you are. I know who you have always been. Let me tell you. Of course, he was entirely wrong about who I was. Out of the three of us, my youngest brother was the saddest, the loneliest, mostly because of the lies he told that kept everyone at a distance, whereas I was the most anxious and outright miserable. My middle brother was moderately happy. My mother once said my youngest brother's lies didn't matter, it was true he loved us, that would always be the truth. When she said that, she broke her own heart. Whereas I once spent my afternoons in a carpeted coffeehouse in downtown Milwaukee, my youngest brother found refuge in the old granary mill, as he had described in I LIKE LIVING HERE. Instead of coming home after school, he was permitted by the local historian Mrs. Kowalski into the mill, where he sat on a wooden bench and sketched in his notebook. Shortly before he died, my youngest brother emailed to ask if I remembered Mrs. Kowalski, if I knew what had happened to her. *I always dreamed about living and working at the mill*, he wrote. *But the granary mill shut down and I don't know where she went.* I imagined my youngest brother walking by the mill in its present condition, and as he peers into its windows, he is astonished at the abundance of dark green plants bursting from beneath the floorboards, overtaking his beloved mill from within. It was rumored that Mrs. Kowalski disappeared. The case remained unsolved. When I looked her up online, I couldn't find any information about her. Not one local news article, not even a blog. Had she existed? Perhaps he had misremembered her last name. Like our mother, he could be forgetful, whereas I remembered almost everything, especially the ways I'd been wronged, every petty grievance. My middle brother never acknowledged his behavior or apologized. And why would he? I never brought it up with him. I never saw myself as a victim, I saw myself simply as an object that happened to be in the room like a lamp, a rug, a painting of blue skies and a bare hill. It was a joke, I could hear him saying to no one. It was just a joke. Touching my legs, it was an accident, his hand simply brushed my legs as he reached for the remote control. A house spider, its yellow translucence, darting back into the crevice. One night as we watched television, I felt something tickle my arm and I thought it was my middle brother's finger; it turned out to be an actual house spider. I was afraid to write about what happened with him; I was afraid people would understand it as an explanation, some kind of traumatic explanation. I was afraid they would not see me as a man, because if I had been a man, my middle brother would not have wanted to touch me. To write was to go back and to move forward. Sometimes there was not much generosity in the act of writing. Sometimes writing was like going to the dentist, which was why I listened to nineties dentist's office music while I wrote. My father in Korea said he had the lifelong sense that I believed I was alone in the world, and he wanted me to know I was wrong, I wasn't alone. I had him, my mother, and three older sisters, one of whom spoke and taught English. Three older sisters, like something out of a fairy tale, I remembered thinking. The three of them are excellent at sewing, I've been told, the three of them are tall, lovely to look at, terrible with money. The three of them have experienced financial ruin but have never asked me for anything, even though out of all of us, I'm the one who has the most money, whereas within my adoptive family, I'm the poorest. When my youngest brother died, he had $6.66 left in his bank account. He once described having detailed, vivid, fantastic dreams of excavating jeweled caverns, flying over lunar surfaces and deserts and ravines and gorges, polar expeditions, etc., whereas my dreams were about teaching, missed deadlines, social infractions. I described these dreams in *Afternoon Hours of a Hermit*, and I was astonished to learn more people weren't interested in them. I didn't know about Matthias's dreams because I never asked him. I have no idea what his dreams are like or if he dreams at all, I reflected, I have no idea if he falls asleep easily or if he has to drug himself. One day I woke up and decided I would wear all white clothing for the rest of the year. One day I woke up and decided to do intermittent fasting. One day I woke up and decided I would title everything I wrote *Afternoon Hours of a Hermit*, even if the title made no sense or didn't suit what I had written, I simply liked the sound of it, a stone dropped down a well. Whereas I was certain Matthias woke up happy and refreshed, my youngest brother and I were disappointed to wake up, not to have died in our sleep, which is the most ideal way to die. Each night, if I pray, I pray only that I won't wake up the next morning, and I'm slightly despondent upon waking that I'm still here. Perhaps what's most important is I have better eyesight than my brothers. It's a fear of mine to go blind because my vision is clear, uncompromised, unsparing. The two of them needed glasses, contacts, lubricants, Lasik, optometrist appointments, so I never understood why my father described my vision of the world as *somewhat foggy*, I'd never in my life needed glasses or contacts or anything to enhance my eyesight, for almost forty years I've had 20/20 vision.

32

Traffic from the mall to my youngest brother's high school was light, even though it was almost rush hour. His high school was less than a mile from The Chocolate Goose. I passed the plaza on Bluemound Road where I would drop off my youngest brother for work at Hollywood Video. I imagined finding him after all these years behind the counter, a lanyard around his neck with a key ready to unlock the clamshell DVD cases. Over the span of a decade, he claimed he was an undergraduate studying criminal justice, a law student, a federal investigator for Homeland Security, and a detective at a police station. How did he keep all of his roles straight? I remembered asking him how it felt to be a detective, and he said it was surprisingly boring. Paperwork, bureaucracy, etc. A boring desk job. I believed what he said, his description of his detective job sounded accurate to me, when it turned out the only job he ever had in his almost thirty years of existence was as a part-time clerk at Hollywood Video.

As I drove to his high school and listened to the classical music station on the radio, I envisioned a large auditorium smelling of teenage sweat and pencil erasers, with dark red dust-covered velvet curtains and a podium with a spotlight operated by a student A/V crew. The dimness of the auditorium would make it easy for me to walk up the steps on the side of the stage to the podium and begin my reading unannounced. I banked on the fact that the audience members would be too Midwestern, too polite, to disrupt my reading. Perhaps the person who had sent me the threatening smiley face letter and detective photo would be in the audience. It was simple, I thought, my setup was so simple. All I had to do was draw out the ones who once knew my youngest brother and his *constellation of women*. After the reading, I would take them aside and I would interrogate them.

I pulled into the parking lot of my youngest brother's high school, a six-story cream-colored brick building. There were signs with arrows that said READING TONIGHT throughout the Pope Pius hallway and leading up a slate gray marble staircase. After I followed the signs up four flights of marble steps, I found myself standing in the back corner of a brightly lit conference room within the library of Pope Pius High School.

There were seven or eight people, around my parents' age or older, seated, spread out across round conference tables. All the overhead fluorescent lights were switched on as if someone were about to teach a continuing education class. The people seemed to know one another. I heard them talking about what a disappointment last week's reading was.

A small, nervous-looking woman in a bright pink sweater entered the room and walked up to the podium with a microphone and asked the people to consolidate to one or two tables at the front of the room. I stood in the back with my arms folded.

Sir, would you like to come up here as well? said the woman at the podium. Don't be shy. Yes, you in the sunglasses and baseball cap, she continued. Standing alone in the back in the corner . . . Sir, we're not going to get started until you come up to the front of the room with us.

Everyone seated at the tables turned around to watch me walk reluctantly about twelve paces to a spot at an empty table. As I walked, I could hear the elderly breathing. They seemed to want to know what I was doing there, but were too polite and reserved to make formal, outright inquiries. I was disappointed not to see anyone who could possibly be from my youngest brother's class; the ones who were living and breeding in the suburbs of Milwaukee had not bothered to show up yet.

The small, nervous-looking woman at the podium said her name was Millie Baker. Millie asked everyone to say hello to an even smaller woman, Sister Matilda Pierre, a Dominican nun, who was standing next to her.

A nun, I thought, that's strange.

It was too late to say, I'm sorry, this is a mistake, I was not meant to be here. Goodbye, have a nice night. Enjoy your reading with Sister Matilda Pierre, I've had an emergency come up.

There was no way for me to leave.

Not now.

As Millie patiently read the nun's biography and the fifteen different titles of Sister Matilda Pierre's self-published poetry works, Sister Matilda looked out at the audience with a wise, knowing gaze. One of the elderly yawned and then another. Several more people came into the room, some around my age. Possibly the ones who could've been my youngest brother's classmates. Perhaps they were now teachers at the school. How would I identify the ones who knew and loved my youngest brother?

The featured writer, Sister Matilda, said she wanted to try something new and instead of reading poetry, she would read from a long essay she was working on. Approximately four or five minutes into her reading, an audience member asked her to speak more directly into the microphone and to slow down. She changed the pace of her speaking, which I estimated would extend her reading by at least five or six minutes. A little later, she asked Millie Baker for a glass of water. Millie apologized for not thinking of that. She said she never forgot to offer readers a glass of water, she had no idea what had come over her that night. Perhaps something was distracting her, she said. Sister Matilda said it was fine. When she stopped to drink water, she sipped loudly into the microphone. When she ran out of water about three quarters of the way through the reading, she asked Millie for a fresh glass.

Sister Matilda stood at the podium in total silence as Millie stepped out into the hallway to get more water. It was so quiet as the sister-poet stood there alone at the podium, I could hear the buzzing of the overhead lights, and I was reminded of taking a standardized test in high school and how I never wanted to be the first to finish or the last; it was best to finish somewhere in the middle, to blend into the background the way my youngest brother had blended in with the beige wall. Of course, there are times when it can be a problem to blend in too much, I reflected, as I remembered in second grade my family moved to the suburbs of Milwaukee from the suburbs of Chicago a month after school had already started. My homeroom teacher did not acknowledge my presence until more than a month later. Why didn't you tell me you were here? she said, astonished, panicked. She flipped through the pages of her attendance ledger, her eyes widening. You never said a word to me. I don't know you or how you ended up here. Who are you? What's your first and last name, honey? It became clear to me and everyone else in the classroom, approximately thirty children, that she had mixed me up with the other Asian, Huan Lin, and thought we were the same person.

The reading went on for more than forty minutes but was contemplative in tone, as Sister Matilda described various accounts of a bleeding woman, a man with dropsy, an orphan, a woodcutter with a broken foot, etc., all who had been healed by coming into physical contact with Jesus. At the end Sister Matilda requested we join in a prayer. An older man reached for my hand, and I could feel how small mine was engulfed in his, calloused, warm, and hairy, the hand of a construction worker or farmer. I thought of my mother holding my youngest brother's hand in the hospital.

His withered red apple.

When the prayer was over, the nun asked if anyone had any questions. The room became quiet again and I heard a new person yawn. Sister Matilda said she would appreciate if at least one person would ask her a question, since to ask a question shows you're interested in what you've just spent more than forty minutes listening to, and if you don't ask the author a question, it feels like the reading was a total waste of time for everyone, author and listener. The audience members looked around the room or down at the floor. Someone began to speak but only to the person sitting next to them.

Millie Baker came to Sister Matilda's rescue and appeared at the podium and said we should give Sister Matilda a round of applause and that some of her self-published works were available for sale tonight. We clapped, and Sister Matilda and Millie left the podium for one of the conference tables set up with her books. People started to rise from their seats. It was now my turn to go up to the podium and speak, and although I was an unexpected guest, perhaps even an unwelcome one, I knew I had to, because it was possible someone in the room once knew my youngest brother and could tell me about him, specifically about the names of the women he had written on his hand or the troubled woman who had covered her face at the funeral.

It was also possible some people in the audience were expecting me to read, based on the promises of my email invitation. The local author who had published one book. My hands were sweating. My cheeks flushed dark red. I could feel the blotches burning up. I had already sweated through the armpits of my new shirt, the pale blue one with a collar like what my youngest brother once wore. The patches of sweat underneath my armpits were impossible to conceal even if I kept my arms rigid and close to my body. I had to do this reading, I thought, there was no other way to get what I needed. I took off my sunglasses, cleared my throat, went up to the podium, and began to speak into the microphone, taking everyone in the room by surprise.

33

I forgot to bring my book. I could've read from my phone but didn't have time to search my inbox for a PDF of my novel. My hands were sweating, my throat was dry. Without thinking about it, as if guided by some external force, I explained I was a detective who had reopened his investigation after new material had come to light. I said there were three names written on my youngest brother's hand the night he died in the hospital. A name on each finger, I know it sounds odd, I said, I know it sounds peculiar, but he wrote a name on his index, middle, and ring fingers. The names looked like black caterpillars trembling on his hand, coming to life.

Although my voice was wavering, suggestive of the fact that my investigation was intensely emotional for me to speak about in public, I could see that the audience members admired my composure. I might have even seen a single tear slide down an old woman's cheek, she was so moved by what I was saying. I had only just begun to outline the exact circumstances of my brother's death, *his suicide*, and I could already tell I was winning over several people in the audience. I remembered from my teaching experience that it was helpful for students to have a visual aid; I took out the photo of my brother dressed up as a detective.

This photo of my dead brother was sent to me days ago in an envelope without a return address. If you look closely at it, you can see my brother's eye of inquiry—

Sir, I really need you to step away from the microphone, Millie Baker interrupted from somewhere in the back of the room. Step away!! Now!!

Everyone turned around. With an expression of disbelief, she walked quickly toward the front of the room where I was standing. She took great strides up to the podium and yanked my upper arm even though she was smiling politely, a very tight, rigid, Catholic, Midwestern smile I was familiar with from my childhood in the suburbs of Milwaukee. I was embarrassed when I felt her fingertips graze the patch of sweat on my shirt.

You can't do this, she hissed in my ear as she went on smiling. This is not a free-for-all open-mic salon.

Listen, I'm sorry, everyone, about this, this disruption, she said into the microphone. Please go on and enjoy your evening. And don't forget to donate to our alumni fund.

Anger rose inside me. Because of my youngest brother's connection to the high school and possibly to some of the people in the audience, I felt I, the local author and detective, had every right to be there.

Not only in the room but at the podium.

Thank you for clarifying, Millie, I said into the microphone. But I'm certain some people might have attended this reading expecting to hear me read tonight. Did anyone come to hear me, Dan Moran, read tonight?

The conference room was silent except for a middle-aged man and woman whispering in the back; they appeared to be having a private discussion. It occurred to me the audience members might be too shy to raise their hands, just as they had been too shy to ask the nun any questions.

Don't be shy, as Sister Matilda said—

Sir, I'm going to call security if you don't step away from the microphone right now, she said.

I put my hands up in the air in frustration and resignation. I had seen a very famous actor, hailed as one of the finest actors of his generation, at a café in the West Village raise his hands like that after the barista announced the café had run out of gluten-free cookies. Now that I was away from the microphone and standing next to a conference table with a platter of cheese and crackers, perhaps people would feel less anxious about answering my question.

Sorry to interrupt again, I said, but did anyone come to the reading tonight to hear me read?

The idle chatter in the room tapered off into a remarkable silence.

No, someone said.

Well, I said, if anyone did come to hear me read tonight, please meet me in the hallway.

As I looked out on the small crowd, I saw my cousin Fran pressed between the middle-aged man and woman who had been whispering in the back of the room.

Fran? I called out.

What was he doing here? How had he found out about my reading? A blond woman blocked my view; I lost sight of him. Somehow my cousin Fran had escaped my observation. He had disappeared. I stepped out into the hallway, and I leaned against the pale blue metal lockers, waiting for the teeming masses who would want to talk with me. Someone's leather purse brushed against my shoulder. An older woman stopped in front of me, touched my forearm, told me both her mother and father had committed suicide, told me good luck with everything. I overheard a person remark to their friend that I looked too young to be an actual detective. *i just saw you, where did you go?!!* I texted my cousin Fran. Millie Baker rushed by; she was on the phone, probably trying to hustle someone's contact information for the alumni network. As I tried to make eye contact with the people who might have known my youngest brother, I became aware of the nun standing right next to me who said, Did you say your brother went to school here?

His name was Kevin Moran, I said.

And when did he go to school here, my dear? Sister Matilda asked.

I had to think about it. I did some calculations in my head.

I guess it would be almost twenty years ago, I said.

When I said the words *almost twenty years ago*, I realized my terrible mistake, the error in my logic, its monstrosity.

What's that? she said.

Almost twenty years ago, I tried to tell Sister Matilda, but the words got caught in my throat, dried up, turned on their side in the fetal position, died.

Did you say something? she said. Are you okay, dear?

Could it really have been almost two decades since he had tried to avoid wandering these halls and sitting in these classrooms? What had I been thinking? I could feel myself smiling strangely; Sister Matilda smiled strangely in return. I felt dampness underneath my arms. How ice-cold those wet patches of my shirt had become when they grazed my skin.

Fast-flowing rivulets down the sides of my shirt. Oh, what a failure this is, I admonished myself. How could I have expected people to attend a reading for someone they may have known or sat next to in a classroom or passed by in a hallway twenty years ago? People will rarely attend a reading for a person they know and care about in the present, much less the sibling of a dead person they knew two decades ago.

Kevin Moran, she said, was in my freshman social studies class. A very cute Chinese boy.

. . .

He stood out naturally because there were no other Chinese at this school, she said. You know, now that I think about it, I can count on my hand how many Chinese students there have been here since. Kevin Moran was quiet and did his homework. The first task I assign in freshman social studies is for the students to keep a record of every social interaction they have for a week. I remember your brother was the only student I've had in twenty years who recorded speaking to family members and the bus driver, Brother Terrance, and no one else. Not one other person!! Later, instead of going outside for lunch, he sat with me in my classroom. When I suggested he go outside with his friends, he would protest and say he preferred to stay indoors. After a while I would ask him to do things like wash the chalkboard or tidy the cabinets or organize and dust the bookshelves so he would feel helpful. He seemed to like feeling helpful doing his little tasks more than he liked eating with his friends. I remember seeing him walk down the hall and thinking, That little Chinese boy is so sweet. How is he doing these days?

. . .

Are you okay, dear?

I had difficulty managing an answer for Sister Matilda, I didn't know where to begin. Something inside me was unspooling, a thread from the past, something I hadn't wanted to think about for a long time, *that little Chinese boy*, I was murmuring to myself, those four words had unraveled a thread I had set aside and wanted to forget.

A dark gray thread.

I turned away from the nun and thought, Yes, *that little Chinese boy*, that's what my mother's lifelong best friend and neighbor Judy Luther had called my youngest brother. My mother admitted to me she herself did not once correct Judy Luther as she didn't want to upset her or cause a rift between them; those four words paralyzed my mother, rendered her mute, unable to speak, unable to make a correction. During the post-suicide phase, my mother admitted it was one of her regrets, it was sincerely one of her life's greatest regrets, not to have spoken up, to have permitted Judy Luther to refer to my youngest brother as *that little Chinese boy*, my brother, who had befriended Judy Luther's son. For almost thirty years. Judy Luther called my youngest brother *that little Chinese boy*, as if he had never grown up, she infantilized him, she made him small, in her mind he was so small he didn't need a name, what's the purpose of a name when one can simply call him what he is, that little Chinese boy, whereas her own son would get a job, buy a house, and go on to breed, that little Chinese boy was stuck in limbo, trapped in perpetual boyhood, she never uttered his name, not once, not even the day after he died, the day my mother called her best friend to tell her the news, Judy Luther didn't use his name, my mother told me while I sat on the couch in the post-suicide phase. Judy Luther said she would pray for him, she said she would keep that little Chinese boy in her thoughts and prayers, my mother told me as her hand, arthritic from decades of sewing and embroidery, reached out for mine, seeking some kind of solace from me for the first time in years, perhaps the first time in my life. I'm sorry, she said, and I don't know if she was saying she was sorry to me or to my brother, but I held it, her own withered red apple, for what seemed like an eternity, pressed between my hands, evening falling so fast, my childhood home sinking into darkness, neither of us dared to stand up and turn on a light. And I remembered I did not feel sad for my Korean adoptee brother, I did not feel sad for my mother, I felt only disgust, disdain, rage, a welling up of violence in my stomach, a stabbing pain I wanted to transfer onto someone else, I wanted to find Judy Luther's son and run over him with my brother's black Honda Accord, my brother's deathmobile. No, unlike my mother, I did not feel sad at all, I wasn't sobbing, I was not a sibling who sobbed, I did not feel sorry for myself, I did not feel sorry for my brother or my mother or anyone, I only wanted justice for my brother Kevin Moran, I only wanted to do him justice.

34

Before I left Pope Pius High School, a tall, friendly-appearing man in a navy nylon jacket asked me who I was.

He told me to stand with my back to the row of lockers and requested to take my photo. Perhaps this tall man in the nylon jacket was a journalist for the high school newspaper. I asked Sister Matilda if she wanted to be in the photo, but she declined. She admitted she was shocked when I explained my youngest brother had killed himself with an elegant and methodical plan. That wasn't what she had expected to hear after she asked how the little Chinese boy had turned out, no, not at all, and I thought she might offer to pray for him or at least light a candle in his memory, but she didn't, perhaps because he had committed suicide and was, in her eyes, a mortal sinner.

The man in the nylon jacket was smiling as he took my picture, and I assumed he was going to interview me about my reading, I assumed he had heard I was a local writer and a detective and had questions for me such as, Would you mind speculating on the future of literature for Korean adoptees? How does it feel to be a trans writer in today's cultural landscape? How does your work as a detective overlap with your writing process? Your brother killed himself five years ago and somehow you're the one who's still around. How is that? I was shocked when instead the man in the nylon jacket introduced himself as the assistant head of security, wrote my name down on a clipboard, and told me that even though I appeared to be a nice man, even though he had enjoyed certain aspects of my reading, I was never to return to the grounds of Pope Pius High School or he would be forced to call the police.

35

Sometimes I had the sense I was in two places at the same time. I thought of the woman with the white braid and her paintings. A face layered on top of another face, a preordained face. Every Korean adoptee has a second life simultaneously unfolding in an alternate dimension; I could have had a life in Korea as an authentic Korean with Korean parents I resembled, and my sisters, my three biological sisters who remained in Korea, my three magical fairy-tale sisters who liked to sew. And how lucky I was that one of them spoke English; she was an English teacher who, in her free time, liked to embroider small pillows for people's pets to rest upon. When I told her I, too, was a teacher and a mentor for troubled youth, she said we came from a long lineage of peasants and educators. That makes perfect sense to me, I remembered thinking, as that's exactly what an adjunct instructor is, a cross between a peasant and an educator.

As a Korean adoptee, I had always been split in two.

A part of me that night was already at my childhood home, sitting down at the dining room table with my relatives for my youngest brother's memorial dinner, the ostensible reason I had returned to the suburbs of Milwaukee. I could see our driveway filling up with cars. The Chocolate Goose woman running around, frantic. Matthias and Uncle Karl would sneak out in the backyard to vape, to take the edge off before Matthias had to give his speech. I conjured up a sympathetic neighbor or family friend who would look around and say, Where's your daughter, I mean son? Would it be weird to start without him? The other part of me was driving down a wide empty road past the shopping plazas of my youth, certain I knew where I was and how to return to my childhood home. The sky darkened as I waited for landmarks to orient me, hospital, baseball stadium, cemetery, and when they didn't appear, I realized I had merged two different shopping plazas into a single nonexistent one. I didn't know where I was. I was lost.

I had hit a dead end with no new information, no revelations. Not one new clue. Only a dark gray thread I had forgotten about, leading me where?

I looked up my location on my phone and was surprised to see I was only a few blocks from 212 Alexander Lane, the Normandy Village Apartments. It looked different at night with its spotlights and accent lighting. Someone had taken down the yellow banner outside the leasing office advertising the free first month. From the parking lot, I had a direct view into Zachary's apartment. There were no curtains in his kitchen, anyone could view Zachary and his partner through their window, which exuded an intimate yellowish warmth. They were holding hands and talking quietly, a candle between them. I sank down low enough in the driver's seat to go undetected but kept my eyes on them, a picture of domestic tranquility, just visible above the steering wheel.

A minute passed, then Zachary was making animated gestures with his hands. Something the woman said must have upset him. I got out of the car. I decided to sneak up to the window and hide behind the invasive plant so I could eavesdrop again. The night sky was clear with an advancing chill. It is really a beautiful evening, I thought, this night of my brother's memorial dinner. I saw Zachary partner's blow out the candle, and the room went dark. As I crossed the lawn, my phone pulsed. A call from an unknown number. I declined. My phone pulsed again, kept pulsing.

Hello?

Is this ______ Moran? said a masculine voice, strong, confident, clear.

My name is Dan now.

Got it. Listen, what are you doing tonight? What are you doing right now?

Who would want to know these things? I wondered.

Who is this? I said.

Why are you standing outside of my window? said the voice.

As I backed away from the window, I saw a man taking long strides across the grass, making his approach. He had his phone up to his ear.

I see you, he said. Don't go anywhere.

And then an Asian man stood before me.

His Asian face looked into my Asian face, and he said, I've seen you before. I know who you are.

36

I saw you yesterday on Bluemound Road, he said. And later you were spying on us through the window. You're a Moran.

He wasn't angry or hostile. I was surprised he seemed interested in talking.

You remember me, right? he said. Zachary Moon. Do you want to come inside?

Hearing the name Zachary Moon startled me. I had given his name to a minor character in my first book, a helpless person who was nothing like the man standing before me. I'd liked his name, how strange it sounded, but I never gave a thought to the actual person attached to it. I remembered him mostly as a child; he never talked, he never laughed, he blended into the background like my brother. Although it was late and I should've been making my way back to my childhood home, I accepted Zachary's invitation because I thought I could persuade him to admit he was the one who had sent me the threatening smiley face letter.

I know you have many questions that have gone unanswered about a variety of topics near to your heart.

I followed him into his apartment, where a woman, Anna, introduced herself as his wife. The lights were on, and I could smell the smoke from the candle being blown out. As Anna cleared the plates from the kitchen table, I asked him how he had known to call me.

He said he had been thinking of my youngest brother

because of the time of year, and then yesterday, at the intersection, he saw me, and it was like looking at a ghost. Later that day, he called my parents to ask for my number.

Did they say anything about my new name? I said.

No, he said.

I was disappointed but not surprised.

I also called Matthias, he said. We haven't talked in years. He didn't answer. Your brother and I never really liked Matthias.

Zachary said he was sorry to stare, but he couldn't get over how much I now resembled my youngest brother, down to the choice of clothing. The light blue polo shirt. The baseball cap. The sweating.

Of course, he said, your faces are very different. Your brother's face was somber and closed off, yours is lively and animated. I remember when you were ______. You had a bad temper, and you hated driving us around everywhere when we were little. And it was obvious to us from a young age that you were a blatant lesbian, but it wasn't obvious to us back then that you were a man.

Before he went any further, I had to stop and ask if he had sent me a threatening letter.

A letter? I don't even know where you live.

Someone sent this to my childhood home, I said.

He and Anna took turns reading it. Anna said she thought it was a prank. Zachary said he was certain it was a form of religious proselytizing. His mother had received a handwritten letter from someone from the Catholic Church offering to pray for her and to accompany her to a mass. Zachary himself didn't write letters, he couldn't think of the last time he had written someone a letter and dropped it in the mail. I took out the photograph of my brother dressed up as a detective. Zachary said he remembered the day it had been taken. My brother had worn the trench coat to school, and some kids had teased him, they said he looked like an Asian character from a film, others started calling him the character's name, after that he no longer wore the trench. I asked if he knew who took the picture.

Oh, Matthias took it, he said, as if it were obvious.

I was surprised.

Are you sure? I said.

Your mother gave Matthias the camera for his birthday, and he was showing off.

How could Matthias have been the one to see my brother the way he wanted to be seen? I did not believe Matthias had the necessary aesthetic or intellectual ability to capture my youngest brother's eye of inquiry. To hide my disappointment, I pivoted and asked Zachary if he liked living at the Normandy Village Apartments.

It's okay, he said.

He had lived in this apartment for almost seven years, ever since he'd graduated with his degree in physical therapy. I told Zachary I knew my brother had lived here, too. That's right, he said. Somehow, during the last year of my brother's life, Zachary had convinced him to rent an apartment in the same complex.

I want to show you something, he said.

Zachary took out his phone and scrolled through his

images. The winter before he died, he said, my youngest brother took Zachary and their mutual friend Thomas Pon to Las Vegas. On their drive into the city from the airport, my brother asked the taxi driver to pull over, he had a surprise for them. My brother had paid for an electronic billboard to display a Simpsons quote on a highway from the airport to the hotel. What was the quote? I asked Zachary. He said it was an inside joke and I wouldn't understand. Anyway, Zachary said, the taxi driver took a picture of the three of them standing in front of the billboard. Having come from the freezing cold of Wisconsin, they had on button-down shirts, stonewashed jeans, and variations of long black leather jackets, not the biker kind but what an average young man from Wisconsin might find for sale on the racks at Burlington Coat Factory. I was astonished to see my youngest brother smiling in the picture.

He loved to plan grand gestures for people, Zachary said. Sometimes I think he's been hiding this entire time in a place like Korea or Thailand and one day he'll pop up and ask us if we missed him.

I thought this was a dramatic and somewhat romantic notion; it was not one I believed in.

I believed when my youngest brother killed himself, it was final.

Although my youngest brother was smart and strategic, Zachary said he never knew what was real with him, what was imagined, what was an elaborate story or scheme, and it was something he continued to parse out. Sometimes he told himself it didn't matter what was real, it was like listening to a beautiful fairy tale, one could sit back and let the tale take over with no harm to one's integrity in accepting it. Although he wasn't sure if this was cold or unfeeling to admit, he said ultimately what was real or not had no effect on him or the way his own life unfolded.

He admitted there was a lot they didn't discuss. Zachary was half Korean, and he knew Kevin was a Korean adoptee, but they never talked about it.

What about women? I said. Did he talk about any women?

We never discussed that, he said. And I never saw him with one. He probably thought I was asexual, although I thought he was asexual, too.

But when they were in Las Vegas, Zachary did notice my youngest brother would take calls out in the hallway each morning. He assumed they were work-related. One morning Zachary heard my brother's phone ringing while he was in the shower. It was an unlisted number. Out of curiosity, Zachary picked it up and answered. Kevin? said a woman's voice. Who is this? Zachary asked. The woman hung up. He thought it was odd, but he never followed up with my brother about it.

Was her name Sofia? I said. What did her voice sound like? Was it clear or garbled?

I don't remember, he said. It was probably a normal woman's voice.

I asked Zachary if he had ever been inside my brother's apartment, and Zachary said it was odd: even though the two of them lived in the same building, even though they saw each other at minimum once or twice a week, the entire year my youngest brother lived there, Zachary had been inside only once.

What was it was like? I asked.

Zachary ran his hands through his black hair and said he couldn't remember.

You must remember something about it.

Zachary said one afternoon they went to see a movie about a tense and violent hostage situation; they agreed the ending was confusing. Afterward Zachary asked if they could hang out at my brother's apartment so they could keep talking about the movie. My youngest brother had already been living there for months, and Zachary wanted to see how he had settled in. My youngest brother kept putting him off.

It's the same beige walls either way, my youngest brother said, according to Zachary.

But Zachary persisted and forced his way into the apartment, and when my youngest brother finally relented, Zachary was surprised as the cheap hollow door swung open. A completely empty space with nothing inside of it, only the expanse of the beige walls and the vastness of wall-to-wall light brown carpeting.

There was nothing in it, he said. Do you want to see? I took a picture.

. . .

I looked at his phone.

There was nothing in it, I confirmed for myself.

I was surprised my youngest brother had allowed Zachary to see his empty apartment. I wondered if he had hoped Zachary might ask him why his apartment was so empty; I wondered if allowing Zachary to step into the emptiness of his apartment was a prompting of fate to see if someone, his close friend, would notice something was wrong and come to his rescue.

The last week of my brother's life, Zachary said he hadn't heard much from him. One night, after a few days of silence, Zachary called to ask him if he wanted to go to a movie, but my brother said he couldn't. He had gotten into a car accident on Alexander Lane and had broken his leg. He said a friend was already helping him out. A woman. Someone Zachary didn't know.

Was it Sofia? I said.

He wasn't sure, he never saw anyone going in or out of the apartment, not even my youngest brother himself. That week they hardly talked. Zachary knocked on my brother's door a few times and no one answered. He must be recovering, Zachary thought. But it was strange not to hear from him. The night my youngest brother committed suicide, the night I myself lay on the couch and then on the bathroom floor in my studio apartment in Manhattan sick to my stomach with food poisoning, sicker, more nauseated, than I had ever been in my life, that very night Zachary was driving down Wisconsin Avenue heading home from a concert when he saw my youngest brother's car, the black Honda Accord, pulled over in front of the hospital. The streetlamps along Wisconsin Avenue shone brightly, almost as bright as the stadium lights at Miller Park, where the two of them would watch baseball games in silence from the cheapest seats possible. And Zachary knew it was my youngest brother's car because of the 666 license plate, which my Catholic mother constantly harassed him about. Zachary said the car was pulled over on the side of the road, but what was strange was he could see my brother inside, alone, his head leaning against the driver's-side window, deep in thought.

How can he drive if his leg is broken? Zachary wondered.

Zachary drove on. He was listening to the radio, a song he liked but would never admit to liking, Mariah Carey's "Fantasy," and halfway through "Fantasy," he had second thoughts about what he'd seen, some inner voice told him to turn back, some inner voice warned him there was something wrong. Why would his best friend lie to him about having a broken leg? He had never known Kevin Moran to be a liar. He didn't have the right face for lying; Kevin Moran blushed too easily, his cheeks would turn bright red.

Zachary turned around and drove back in the direction of where my brother had parked his car in front of the hospital entrance.

As he drove back toward the hospital, he reconsidered.

You're being overdramatic, he said to himself. Knowing how private my brother was, he decided it would be best if he turned around one final time and went home. He had caught my brother in a lie, but what good would it do to confront him?

If Kevin Moran had lied to him about having a broken leg, there was probably a reason behind it, Zachary reassured himself.

A good reason.

A reason he would discover soon enough.

In all their years of friendship, Zachary had never known Kevin Moran to tell a lie.

Besides, when he thought about it, what he saw as he drove past, simply stated, was a man sitting alone in his car at night.

As soon as Zachary got back to his apartment, around one in the morning, he called my brother's phone and it rang and rang. Zachary left a message saying he saw his car pulled over in front of the hospital. He said he was thinking of him and hoped his recovery was going well. He reminded my brother that he was a physical therapist. He could teach him things to help his recovery go faster.

A silence came over Zachary's apartment. Anna peered into the kitchen from the hallway. I hadn't noticed that sometime during our conversation she had left the room. She said she was going to bed and not to stay up too late. Zachary turned and apologized to me. He said he wasn't used to talking about what had happened that night. He hadn't thought about it in years, and now here I was, asking him to narrate events that were far away from him. He felt he hadn't done a good job explaining what he saw.

Let me go back, he said.

The night my brother parked outside the hospital, the night my brother decided to take his own life, Zachary had turned around and continued home, leaving my brother behind. He said as he did his second and final U-turn on Wisconsin Avenue, Zachary had glanced at my youngest brother's black Honda Accord, and underneath those streetlamps, the ones shining as brightly as the lights at the baseball stadium, he could see through the windows of the black Honda Accord, and with a clarity he had never experienced since that very night, he could see my youngest brother's head tilted down, contemplating something that must have been on his lap, and then for a second, right as Zachary drove past the window, my brother looked up, and the two of them locked eyes.

They locked eyes.

Zachary looked at my brother's face.

. . .

Zachary and I were quiet again and at last I spoke up.

I asked him what my brother's face looked like in that moment.

I wanted to know what he saw.

What he saw in and of my brother's face.

Zachary hesitated.

He said he couldn't say.

For a long time, I had believed I alone was the one closest to my youngest brother, but as I sat across from Zachary, it occurred to me that he was the one who had seen and talked to my youngest brother more frequently than anyone else in his life including my parents and my middle brother Matthias and me. Whereas I was the one who dropped in and out of his life whenever I felt like it, this man, this Zachary, had met with him at least once if not twice each week. Zachary Moon was the one who saw my brother's face moments before he decided to take his own life.

It's weird, Zachary said, and it occurs to me only now, having talked to you, how, throughout the years your brother was working toward his degree or studying for the bar exam or about to drive to Racine to serve a warrant, every weekend and some weeknights he was free to hang out exactly as the two of us did each weekend in middle school and high school. Isn't it strange? He laughed. Isn't it strange how available he was? Don't you find it strange that even though he had all these different elaborate and time-consuming occupations, each weekend we went to a movie, a restaurant, or a casino in downtown Milwaukee? I feel weird saying this now, out loud, but I realize as I'm talking to you, in my life and his, there wasn't one weekend we didn't go to one of those three places. Isn't that strange?

He was laughing.

Upon further reflection, it might have been a clue about what was going on with him, Zachary said, but when you're living your life, you don't search for signs of another person's unhappiness or despair or suicidal thoughts or rage or desperation or hopelessness.

At least I didn't, he said. Did you?

37

I walked to the end of the red-carpeted hall lit by brass lamps illuminating several watercolor paintings of local Milwaukee tourist sites. I entered a narrow stairwell up to the second floor, and from behind some distant door I could hear a man and woman's laughter, the sound of footsteps, then nothing. Outside what was once my youngest brother's apartment door, I stood in silence. Zachary had told me which unit it was. I knocked. It felt the same to me as knocking on any other door. I knocked again, louder. Waited. Then I knocked with the force of the policewoman who had appeared at my parents' door in the middle of the night disrupting their dreams, forcing them down the stairs to receive her news, her life-altering news, the kind of news that rearranges a person, causes them to drop to their knees as I was certain my mother had dropped to hers, although I wasn't physically present with her that moment, the night she received the news of his death, so I couldn't be certain, I would have to ask her, I thought, when the time is right, when the time presents itself, only at the right moment. And then perhaps I would understand everything and be able to move on with my life.

I pressed my ear to the beige door for what seemed like an eternity. Part of me was frozen; I didn't know what I hoped would happen. Did I expect him to answer the door, to reveal himself to me after all these years? And how would I explain myself and who I had turned into? As I continued to press my ear to the door, I swore I could hear a man breathing directly on the other side as if his ear were also pressed against the door, mirroring my position. A man who traveled to far-flung locations only in his head, a gardener of imaginary gardens, a weaver-perfectionist who in his solitude rips apart at night his tapestry of invisible threads. A scene of incomprehensible solitude. I could hear him breathing and I knew he was smiling. I could tell the door itself was cheap and hollow like a small acoustic guitar for a child; whatever it was made of amplified the man's inhalations and exhalations. Then he stopped.

I once asked my Korean adoptee therapist what she thought my youngest brother did all day.

Some people don't do much, my Korean adoptee therapist said. The worst hours are the afternoon ones, the afternoon hours of hermits, that's when I get the most emergency calls.

She laughed, she had made herself laugh.

What do you mean? I said.

Just what I said, ______!! she said somewhat impatiently. Some people don't do much!!

She took a sip of peppermint tea. And she said it with such conviction, I knew it wasn't a vague speculation or hypothesis, I knew she was speaking from real-life situations with her clients, her troubled people must've spoken at length about how they were afflicted with mental ailments leaving them incapacitated and unable to do much with their days.

They go on living until they decide not to.

I was in my brother's car, driving past the leasing office, when I saw the lights were on. I remembered what Zachary had said about a woman who helped my brother with his supposed injury. If she was real, if she existed, maybe the office workers had seen her. I parked and got out. The office was unlocked, so I let myself in. No one was there to stop me from going behind the counter where the woman had stood and lined up the jewels on her phone and exploded them one by one. Underneath the counter was a shelf of three-ring binders labeled by the year. I had negative associations with three-ring binders ever since a well-meaning professor in graduate school suggested I organize my manuscript in progress with a three-ring binder, *the three-ring-binder process*, she called it. I opened a binder and leafed through a history of each unit with the tenants and their leases. I took 2013.

38

As I sank into the driver's seat of my youngest brother's Honda Accord, I flipped through the binder's pages until I came across his name. I examined his application and the lease filled out in his cramped but enigmatic handwriting. He had stated his occupation was law school student.

There was a note stapled to the lease. It was dated September 27, 2013.

Dear Normandy Village Apartments,

I want to make an amendment to my lease. I have three months left which goes through to the end of the year. For these last three months, SH will be staying in my apartment #66. I have paid the rent for the rest of the year in advance.

Here is SH's number (XXX) XXX-XXXX

If any other issues come up here is Mary Moran's number (XXX) XXX-XXXX and my sister ______ Moran's (XXX) XXX-XXXX

Thank you.
Kevin Moran

September 27, I noted, the day before his suicide.

Earlier that night I had asked Zachary about the crying

woman who covered her face at the funeral. I wasn't there, I'm sorry, he said. But people cry at funerals, he continued, a person crying doesn't mean anything. And when I asked him if he detected any signs of hopelessness or despair in the picture of my brother in the brochure, Zachary said not at all, my brother looked like himself.

The smiley face letter, a girlfriend, a woman who covered her face, he had taken my clues and snuffed them out like little candle flames.

At the end of the day, Zachary said, what is it you want to discover?

. . .

He's dead. He's been dead for five years.

I pivoted and asked him about the names on my youngest brother's hand, the three senseless names.

I'm sorry, I don't know how to say it.

Say what?

I hope this isn't rude, he said. But the only women I ever heard him talk about were you and your mom.

As I scanned the note for clues, I noticed a distinct pattern:

SH
Mary Moran
_______ Moran
The three names.
The black caterpillars trembling on his hand.
His withered red apple.

He must've written the three names on his hand as a reminder to himself the day before he died.

All along I had wanted to know what I was to him, and there was my answer: a woman, one of the three women in his life, one of his *female emergency contacts.* Upon reflection, I realized he didn't need to write down my deadname. There was no reason to write my deadname or phone number in his note to the rental office on September 27. At that time I was living and working in Manhattan, overseeing my troubled youth as an after-school supervisor, not yet an adjunct or author. He must have known that I would return to our childhood home immediately after his death, he'd known I would swoop in from Manhattan to descend upon Milwaukee, to enthrone myself on our parents' couch in the living room, to observe everything, to offer my emotional support.

It was strange to see the error of my deadname, that miscalculation of who I was, depicted so clearly, so factually dry, arid, with no emotion or judgment attached to it, the Sahara dryness of my deadname, of who I once was to him, of who I was to everyone. He did not see me. He did not know me. And I had to be at peace with it, with who and what I was to him for almost thirty years. There was no way to change it now. There was no way to change what he knew of me. My biological sister once told me when our mother in Korea was pregnant with me, she had numerous dreams she would give birth to a boy. A beautiful black-haired baby boy. My biological sister said if I had been born a boy, our parents would've kept me, and not only would they have kept me, but as a male,

I would've occupied the most honorable, favorable position in our poverty-stricken family. But because the story went another way, I was destined to plunge them further into poverty, so they chose to give me up, to send me off to an orphanage; there was no way for them to take care of *four females with no future*, and their decision commenced my lifelong sense I was apprehending the world through the eyes of a perpetual other, a mere visitor, an alien beamed down from some dark planet who inhabited not only the wrong body but also the wrong world. When I sent my biological sister a photo of myself standing in front of an old oak tree, arms folded across my chest, not smiling, she wrote, *Are you turning yourself into a man to correct our parents' mistake?* It wasn't true, but on occasion, regarding my biological mother's dreams, I believed certain decisions had been destined all along. The question of what I was would mark me from the moment I was conceived. And shortly after I was born, I would be transported to a new continent where two white Catholics awaited my arrival, and thus I was brought into upper-middle-class Midwestern suburbia where I was raised as a woman. After I made my escape to New York, eventually I became what my biological mother had dreamed of. Unfortunately, my youngest brother would never know these contours of my past, the strange geography of my transition.

Whereas there was no way to change what he once believed about me, what I knew about him was ever evolving, I would never know enough, his life was a blankness as vast as the photo of the empty apartment where he lived the last year of his life. A sweeping beige blankness. To put it plainly, if only he had been able to endure his life for five years longer, he would've watched me transform myself into a male published writer, a male adjunct instructor, a male mentor of troubled youth, a male roommate, a male philosopher of the human condition, a male Moran, and most importantly, a male detective. But there I was, casting myself once again in the starring role, there I was, placing myself at the forefront of the ruins, when it should be about him, only about him, what was important was his life, his death, his name, and although it wasn't right to center myself in his suicide, I couldn't help but ruminate on how he died believing I was a woman, ______ Moran. He never got to see my revision, he never got to meet my final form.

39

Somehow I had overlooked Sofia Hatch and the silent threads she had spun around my brother and his death: the phone call to my childhood home, her entry in his guestbook, her initials in his note. I imagined her, with a last name like Hatch, as a small, blond, youngish woman, sitting in a pew at his funeral, crying, coughing, covering her face, wiping away her tears.

Are you the one behind all of this? I wanted to ask her. Are you the one who sent me the threatening smiley face letter and the photo of my brother dressed up as a detective?

Her number was right there, on his note, taunting me. Before I knew what I was doing, her phone was ringing.

Hello? said Sofia Hatch.

I told Sofia Hatch that although I didn't know her well, I believed we had something in common.

Who is this? she said.

I said that I, too, wished I had known my youngest brother better. I explained I had seen her message in my youngest brother's funeral guestbook and her name in connection to his apartment.

I'd like to know more about you, I said. What was your role in my brother's life? What was so special about your relationship with him? Who are you to him?

. . .

Hello? Are you there?

I'm sorry, she said at last, I'm finding this conversation upsetting. I think it might be best if you don't contact me again. Thank you for understanding.

She hung up. Why didn't she want to talk with me? Had I overlooked something? A beam of light cut across the interior of my brother's car, then my face, interrupting my thoughts and momentarily blinding me. Shocked, I turned away, and I could hear someone pounding on my driver's-side window, forcing me to feel around for the button to lower it, and when I opened my eyes, a small man was looking in.

Good evening, sir, he said. I'm with the Normandy Village security. By any chance, have you seen this man around?

He showed me a grainy photo on his phone that someone had taken from far away of a man crouched below Zachary's window only very slightly obscured by a bush.

A few of our tenants have reported a suspicious Asian male who's been loitering outside people's windows and in the hallways and the stairwells, he said. A creepy guy.

I haven't seen anyone or anything, I said.

He looked at my face and then at the picture on his phone, and I could see he was forming a connection in his head.

What have you been doing here tonight? he said. Any special plans?

My phone pulsed. I glanced down at it.

hey dan, my cousin Fran texted.

what do you mean where did i go? i'm at your parents house

btw an old friend of yours is here to see you!!

are you coming home soon? can we talk?

i need to talk with you

I'm visiting with Zachary Moon, an old friend of mine, I said to the man. He lives here.

The phrase *old friend* was rattling around in my head.

And which unit number does this Zachary Moon live in? the man said.

Forty or forty-one, I said, although I had no idea.

Just let me give your friend Zachary a call, the man said as he stepped away from the car.

Then it dawned on me.

is it NINA? I texted my cousin Fran. *is Nina at the house? what is she doing there??*

The three gray dots appeared on my phone, then disappeared.

I thought about the things Matthias's old friend didn't know about me, the lies I had told Nina about who I was and how I had deceived her. I thought of The Chocolate Goose woman roving around the house and how she believed I was *the normal one.*

Sir, I need to go home, I said to the man. I'm running late for an event.

Hold on, he said. Don't go anywhere.

My brother died five years ago, I explained, tonight is his memorial dinner. He killed himself.

Before the man could respond, without really thinking, I swerved my brother's car out of the parking spot. I have always been an excellent driver. A cautious risk-taker. I could see in the rearview mirror the man shouting after me. I loved driving my brother's car. How could my parents give Matthias my brother's car when he had done nothing to deserve it? I sped out of the Normandy Village Apartments complex, knowing I might never be able to return there. But I had discovered what I needed to know. The streets were wide open, more open than I had ever seen them, and at each intersection I breezed through the yellow lights. It was almost eleven. I could picture The Chocolate Goose woman in her black apron leaning over each guest to clear their plates, shouting orders at her minions to smile, to spread joy in silence, the dark chocolate fountain all dried-up gray and crusted over. As I turned onto my street and arrived at my childhood home, I was surprised and disturbed to find most of the lights were off.

40

All I had to do was step into my childhood home and give my speech, I thought, that was all that was left for me, to share with my family the discoveries I had made since I left 212 Alexander Lane. The results of my newly reopened investigation. Forty-eight hours had passed since my arrival in Milwaukee and I was no longer searching for answers; now I was ready to share them.

The side entrance was locked. A light was on in the kitchen. The Chocolate Goose woman was standing at the sink, probably scrubbing out a pot or pan. I caught her eye, her dark falcon eyes, and I motioned for her to meet me at the entrance. Seconds later, when she opened the door, the sheen of sweat on her forehead made me feel kind and forgiving toward her.

Busy night? I said.

You should have told me what was going on with you, _______, she hissed. You shouldn't have tried to trick me into thinking you were your brother.

The Chocolate Goose woman's face had turned red, out of disgust or embarrassment, I couldn't tell. I wondered what she had revealed to my family, or if she had kept my impersonation of Matthias to herself, just as I had kept her broom-handling demonstration a secret all these years. She took out a handkerchief, blew her nose, then scuttled back into the kitchen, leaving me alone in the mudroom. I could hear a low murmur, a man talking, what sounded like my brother Matthias's voice, muffled as if it were coming through a vent. He must be giving his speech. If that was the case, it would be my turn soon.

I followed Matthias's voice past the kitchen, through the hallway, and into the two-story foyer. The lights were off. The dining room was empty and the living room. I retraced my steps.

Where is everyone? I asked The Chocolate Goose woman.

She didn't bother to look up from the sink as she pointed downstairs.

The basement, I hadn't been in the basement in years, the basement where I would watch television with my brothers, cross-legged on the floor with a pillow on my lap after I cleaned up the kitchen. I opened the door and tiptoed down the carpeted steps. On my way down, I bumped into my cousin Fran.

Dan, he said, where have you been all night?

. . .

Listen, there's this thing that's been bothering me, he said, and I feel like you're the only one left I can talk to about it.

Is this about *Leaving Las Vegas*? I said.

He looked confused.

It's about his suicide letter, he said.

Let's talk later, I said.

But you're the only one—

Later, I said.

I lingered at the bottom of the steps alone, undetected. Uncle Karl was sitting on a beanbag chair next to Aunt Sue, who had perched herself on the edge of an ottoman. I didn't see Nina anywhere; had my cousin Fran been mistaken? My parents sat on the couch, Matthias's wife and daughter wedged between them. Some cousins were on the floor, lazing around like on a Christmas morning. My middle brother Matthias was holding court in the center of the room with his laptop connected to the TV.

Does everyone remember this? he said.

He clicked on his laptop and a picture appeared: my family and relatives outside a Chinese restaurant captioned *September 28, 2015*. All of them had on the same ugly sweaters, brightly colored tube-shaped sweaters, in an attempt at synchronized happiness and good cheer, even my father who worshipped neutral colors was wearing one. And where was I at the time? September 28, 2015, I must have been writing about them. Instead of joining my family's gathering, I had been in New York studying with Thomas Bernhard, drinking too much coffee, and putting the finishing touches on my manuscript. All these years I had been writing about them!!

My mother saw me, smiled, and waved me over.

Come sit with us, she called out from across the room, but I remained where I was.

Matthias was saying these annual family gatherings were so special, they almost made up for the fact of my youngest brother's unexpected death, his *unexpected death*, he kept saying. Not one word was said about the harsh reality of his suicide. I saw Matthias glance at me and I was disturbed by the hint of sadness I saw on his face.

I wondered what he saw when he looked at me.

I knew I wanted contradictory things, I wanted to go forward, I wanted to forget about how these people once knew and perceived me as ______ Moran, I wanted to move on, and yet I didn't want to forget what had happened with my brothers.

Over here!! my mother said.

Matthias's wife made a great show of getting up and finding a new place to sit.

My mother patted the empty seat next to her.

The couch patterned in a swamp-green paisley with webs and tangles of dark creeping vines, where during our childhood, my middle brother had touched me, now my mother wanted me to sit with her on that couch. To her it was simply a couch, a couch like any other couch, a couch that every once in a while required reupholstering and *freshening up* with sacks of shredded memory foam, that old couch in the basement where she did her sewing as she listened to music from the fifties and sixties on her CD boom box, the good old days, the simple days, it could not be the couch where her son on a regular basis for at least a year had tormented *her beloved once-daughter.* Now my mother wanted me, a middle-aged man, to sit next to her and listen dutifully to her son talk about her other son who was dead. She would never go on to acknowledge she had THREE SONS, I thought, she would always think of me as her daughter, even though it could be said that *her beloved once-daughter* was also now dead. So many dead people with us here in the basement, I said to myself, stifling a laugh as I continued to stand at the bottom of the steps and observe everything. She wanted me to pretend that what had occurred between my middle brother and me was a misunderstanding, perhaps it had been a mistake, I could hear her say to me on the phone years ago, hadn't I ever made a mistake and wished I could take it back? Perhaps it didn't happen, she suggested, perhaps I was misremembering. Perhaps he had been reaching for the remote. You used to hog the remote, you used to make us watch that show about the old man detective, Columbo, but everyone loved *Murder, She Wrote*, no one liked *Columbo.* After all these years it was clear what I'd told her about Matthias had never been properly digested or absorbed. And I remembered how much I once loved my mother, how I adored her, when I was little I would beg her to divorce my father, even back then there was a selfish tiny man inside me waiting to burst out, I wanted her all to myself, I didn't know she would one day sit on the couch upstairs and tell me what her friend Judy Luther had called my brother after he killed himself, what she had permitted Judy Luther to call him; that night, five years ago, she had apologized, then she held my hand and said, It's okay, ______, it's all going to be okay. Her apologies were boundless, but they were never what I wanted to hear from her. She didn't believe me when I told her about Matthias, it's possible she simply couldn't. Foggy vision, I could hear my father saying, you've always had foggy vision.

Why won't you sit here with us? my mother said.

Just as Matthias had softened my brother's suicide into a neutral event, *an unexpected death*, my mother had softened and massaged the couch into a neutral piece of furniture. Without a word, I turned around to sneak back upstairs and withdraw into my childhood bedroom. I could hear Matthias saying how in 2017 everyone got food poisoning, but that wouldn't happen this year thanks to The Chocolate Goose woman. Everyone laughed. Suddenly, halfway up the stairs, I heard my mother call out for me, Wait, wait, wait, come back, ______, don't you have anything you want to say? And there it was, it was my turn to speak, it was my turn to share with them my findings about my youngest brother, findings that began with 212 Alexander Lane and ended with Sofia Hatch, *findings that were existential and philosophical and emotional in nature*, but my mother, she was calling out the wrong name.

41

Thomas Bernhard once told me that characters don't get tired, characters don't get hungry, they don't shit or piss, characters are *puppets made of words*. I thought I had seen him, *my old friend*, my mentor, my writing salvation, sitting in an armchair tucked away in the corner, and I swore I heard him say, from somewhere in the depths of that shitty basement, Your parents are not that bad. They seem simple but normal.

42

September 29, I listened to a voicemail from David Dunn: I worked for your parents for a few days back in 2013. The case didn't go far because they told me to stop, my services weren't needed anymore. I guess some people don't want to know things, they don't want to know the truth. But yeah, I just checked and Sofia Hatch lives downtown: 2211 Prospect Avenue, Unit 3. I found it in the White Pages.

It was early in the evening when I pulled up to a shabby apartment building painted dark blue. Sofia Hatch lived on the East Side, far from the vast suburban blankness of the Normandy Village Apartments. I buzzed Unit 3 but no one answered. I had nothing else to do so I sat in the driver's seat and waited. I was parked on the street, crammed between cars, less than a block from her front door. A few hours passed. That night, like any night, I was alone until a woman came around the corner and walked toward me. The streetlamps illuminated her white hair, a long braid trailing down her left shoulder like a soft white rope. As she approached my brother's car, a few feet away, her blurred features came into focus.

I was astonished to see she was Asian like me, like my brothers.

It hadn't occurred to me that a person with the name Sofia Hatch would turn out to be a Korean woman.

What was a name but a ridiculous costume we must endure the rest of our lives?

And in an instant, I envisioned Sofia Hatch at my brother's funeral. She was crying and covering her face. A man next to her offered her a tissue and she wiped her face and composed herself. Her dark eyes became clear and alert. She was looking around. It took her a moment to realize she was the only Asian person in attendance at this funeral for a Korean adoptee. A little later, just as he'd willed, she would move some of her things into his empty apartment for a few months. She would fill it with the ugliest amateur paintings possible, paintings of people with tangles of yellow hair, yellow teeth, and flashing neon-green eyes that she would find in the neighborhood's thrift stores and lug back to my brother's apartment, where she would paint on top of whatever she had found an Asian face, dark eyes, dark hair, a slender line for a mouth. Never smiling. I imagined her working from noon to night, taking breaks to look out at the parking lot where there was nothing. She had never had a real studio before and my youngest brother's apartment had good light in the afternoon, perfect for her work, which consumed her, hour after hour she would spend painting, and by the time the lease was up, she had covered the beige walls of his apartment with the faces of Korean adoptees.

I rolled down the passenger-side window and leaned over as she walked past my brother's car.

Hi, Sofia, I said quietly. I'm Kevin Moran's brother, do you remember him?

She glanced at me and I sensed she was afraid.

. . .

She didn't stop.

She was turning toward her apartment, steps away from the entrance.

I have some questions about your role in his life, I said. Can we talk?

Silence.

She didn't turn around. She stood facing the entrance and took out her keys. Not even one glance back. She unlocked the door and was gone.

Was it possible she hadn't recognized me?

Perhaps I shouldn't have been surprised.

After all, there was no reason why she should stop to speak to the strange man who had whispered her name in the dark.

I drove off. I had filled the tank like my father instructed me to, but I wasn't going back. My youngest brother's car, which I decided was now my car, would take me wherever I needed to go. As I passed the hospital where he died, where he called them and told them what he was about to do, where Zachary Moon had driven by not once but twice, I saw a black Honda Accord pulled over to the curb, I slowed down, came to a rolling stop, and peered into the driver's-side window, and I saw my brother and he looked at me, I saw his face, which is not sharp like a carving but soft and round like his Korean mother's, and we locked eyes, his eyes are small dark pebbles at the bottom of a clear pond, and I understood I was inside a story, a story someone had told me, and if there was a way out, it had to be written as simply and as quickly as possible, without embroidery or decoration, a simple account of what I saw and what I came to know. I gripped the wheel, leaned forward, and kept going.

Acknowledgments

This book contains a partial quote from Thomas Bernhard's *The Loser,* translated by Jack Dawson (New York: Penguin, 1991), on page 119: "*My constant curiosity got in the way of my suicide*, so he said, I thought."

. . .

Thank you to the early readers of this book and all of my writer friends who have helped me; it's a gift to be in conversation with you.

. . .

A huge thanks to everyone at Ecco, especially Deborah Ghim, for your tremendous guidance. My deepest thanks to Kate Johnson and everyone at Wolf Literary. For their support in the UK, thank you, Stefan Tobler and everyone at And Other Stories. Thank you, Rita Bullwinkel and Amanda Uhle. Thank you to my colleagues at DU, especially Joanna Howard. Thank you, Selah Saterstrom and Amina Cain. Thank you to the Whiting Foundation. Thank you to my family, the Gerards, especially Sarah (my love), Franny, Lora, and Juan.